NO REINS
By
Angie Skelhorn

CHAPTER ONE

"**A**NGEL, TURN OFF THE television and go to bed. You have school in the morning," her mother called from the kitchen.

"Okay...okay." she yelled from the den. She scrambled to her feet from the couch.

In front of the picture window she stopped. An immense glow from the headlight beams came up the laneway. The pickup truck and trailer parked. The headlights shut down. Both the driver and passenger doors opened and then slammed shut. Minutes passed when the front door swung open.

Angel approached the dining area. She stood in the archway between the two rustic rooms dimly lit from the corner table lamps. Her mother wrapped her arms around her son, hugging him close. She cupped his face in her pudgy hands, her eyebrows arched.

"You look tired, Tim. You've aged beyond your nineteen years. Stay and get some sleep," she said.

Tim pulled away from his mother's grip. "I'm fine. I can't stay. The horses in the trailer need to be in Sudbury for the stake races tomorrow. The animals need to rest from the long drive," he said, walking toward the kitchen.

He opened the fridge and removed two cans of pop. "Mom, this is Stephen. He's stabled beside me at the track," he said, returning to the dining area. "His parents own a flower shop."

A man the same age as her son and well-built, stepped from the foyer. He handed Angel's mother a bouquet of blooming white roses.

"They're beautiful, thank you," she gasped, smelling the petals.

"You're welcome," he said with a strong French accent.

* * * * *

ANGEL DIDN'T MOVE. SHE listened to his syllables roll over his tongue completely enchanted by him, wearing his worn, black leather jacket, rich blue sweat shirt and boot-cut jeans. Weak in the knees, her eyes covered every detail; his curly dark hair, bright blue eyes that sparkled, and dark tan. All the little parts that made up the whole.

"Hey, little sister, how's things?" Tim asked. Stephen turned and looked at her, running his hands over his black curls, and smiled.

"Good," she managed to say, feeling a surge of warmth rise in her cheeks.

"When will you come home again, son?" his mother asked, setting the bouquet on the dining table.

"I don't know, mom, but I will call." Tom kissed his mother on the cheek. He walked to the front door, turned the knob and left. Stephen followed. He hesitated for a moment in the entryway, glanced at Angel and smiled, but didn't say anything.

She stared back as he closed the door behind him.

Her mother walked across the hardwood floor toward her and entered the den. Angel joined her at the window and looked out. Beneath a bright, full moon, Tim climbed into the driver's seat while Stephen sat on the passenger's side of the pick-up truck. Both shut their doors.

Tim slid the vehicle into gear, curved the truck and trailer around the circled driveway and crawled down the gravel lane. The headlight beams faded into the dark night as the vehicle drove away.

Angel walked to the dining area and plucked a white rose from the bouquet resting on the table. She ran up the stairs and into her bedroom. She fell into bed and sniffed the flower's wonderful scent wondering if Stephen, too, experienced the same spark as she did. She didn't know how their paths would cross again, or when, only their paths would.

CHAPTER TWO

Eᴀʀʟʏ SUMMER, A YEAR AND a day later, Angel's mother entered her daughter's bedroom. "Up and at it!" she said, opening the curtains to allow the morning light in.

Angel lay in bed and pulled the covers over her head exhaling a defeated moan.

"You can't spend another gorgeous day hiding under the sheets. There's been a dramatic change in your personality. Your mood and attitude changes from one day to the next," her mother said, her hands planted on her hips.

Angel peeked out from under the covers at her mother wearing a denim shirt and white jeans, step over the mess of clothes scattered on the floor. She sat on the edge of her daughter's bed. "Today Jake is hauling a horse to Quebec for Tim. Do you want to go?" she asked, stroking her daughter's bed-head hair.

She sat straight. "I want to go!" she beamed.

"Are you sure? It's a long distance to travel."

"Yes, mom," Angel said, hugging her tight.

Her mother stood, pulled the covers off her daughter. "Okay then, young lady, get up and get yourself dressed," she ordered, smiling.

Angel showered, slid open the dresser drawers and found white socks, underwear and a bra. She twisted and turned from side to side as she admired her small breasts and tanned legs, wearing a white tank top and short, black, Daisy Duke shorts. She thought to herself if *Stephen won't come to me, I'll go to him* as she packed some clean clothes, a twenty dollar bill and loose change into her school knapsack. She stepped over the clutter on the floor, raced down the stairs, through the kitchen and dining area, out the front door, across the gravel drive, into the pick-up truck, and buckled up, full of anticipation at what would come.

A gust of wind encircled the wind chimes hanging from the roof and they chimed above Jake and his mother as they stood on the front porch.

"I made you and your sister a light snack for the ride," she said, handing him a brown paper bag.

"Thanks, mom," he said, walking into her arms, and she hugged him.

Jake jumped into the driver's seat, buckled himself in, put the key into the ignition, turned the engine on, and then slowly pulled away from the main house.

"Have a safe trip," their mother called after them, waving goodbye.

Angel took a quick look at the horse farm in the side-view mirror before the pick-up truck and trailer turned left out the laneway, down the long tree-lined gravel road, past the new sprouts of growth in the corn fields, and then onto the main highway. She watched her past turn into a speck behind her, knowing where she wanted to be, and now the journey had begun.

As Jake and Angel traveled across country, she sat back in her seat, relaxed, and stared out the window at the scenery passing by, consumed with thoughts of Stephen and herself. Angel replayed the same vivid dream, a realistic experience that recurred when she slept. They stood face-to-face, looking at one another in silence. Stephen's hand rested on the middle of her back, her arms around his neck. In his arms, her heart pounding, she sank into him. With his lips on hers she melted from his passionate kiss. In her mind and heart she had fallen in love. She couldn't forget the vision when she woke.

She battled with herself. Logically, she knew she should let the thought of them together go; emotionally she couldn't.

Hours passed as Jake drove, keeping his eyes on the road. They chatted while listening to the music playing on the radio.

Finally, on the outskirts of the French-speaking city, a large bilingual sign read, HARNESS RACING. Jake put on the signal light and turned down the long laneway preparing for the speed bumps ahead. He put the brakes on at the guard shack.

"ORC numbers?" a man with a full head of white hair, wearing a dark blue uniform asked, walking to their pick-up truck. Once he added their personal information to a sheet attached to a clipboard he held, he returned the licenses, and then waved them in. Past the security checkpoint spruce, cedar, pine and birch trees surrounded the back stretch. A fresh layer of stone dust had been laid on the oval-shaped five-eighths track. The two moved along at a snail's pace between eight to ten even rows of quality wood horse barns painted Indian red. Jake pulled the truck and trailer to the side of a barn, hopped out of the driver's seat and stretched. Angel opened the passenger door and stepped onto the loose gravel, easing the door shut behind her.

"Thought I heard a vehicle. How was the drive, Jake? Tim asked, walking around the corner of the building with Stephen beside him.

"The traffic was pretty heavy," he answered, smiling.

Angel stood weak in the knees. She fought to keep her legs strong. Electricity shot through her watching Stephen walk along behind her brother. Good looking, tan skin, dark, curly hair cut short, with piercing ice-blue eyes, wearing a clean, white short sleeve shirt and camouflage knee-length shorts. *Handsome and well dressed*, she thought.

Stephen glanced at her and smiled, walking to the back of the trailer. Jake slid the locks open, pulled the two top, thin doors apart, and then gently dropped the heavy ramp to the ground.

"Good girl," Tim said to the horse, stepping into the trailer through a side door. He looped a lead-chain over the animal's nose and snapped the clip to the metal ring of the stable halter. With patience he backed the large horse out of the trailer.

Jake patted the large animal on her strong neck. "Forever Yours has been a nice condition horse. I hope you can train her down to race in the Free-For-All, Tim," he said.

"You really think this horse has that in her?" he asked.

"She'll do better here. You can work her quite different from what she encountered at the farm."

Tim led the horse toward the barn entrance. Angel followed close behind Stephen, breathing in his intoxicating cologne. Jake strained to slide the large wooden door of the Indian red building open.

Tim positioned the horse on a long, black mat that ran down the center of the barn. He hooked the horse between the crossties. Stephen crouched and ran his hand up and down the horse's leg. He stopped at the ankle. "Great, there's no heat," he said in a thick, French accent.

Angel sat on a large wood trunk resting on the dirt floor and surveyed her surroundings. There were more trunks, some wood, others metal, on either side of the stalls against the walls, with personalized stable logos and at the end of the shed row, two wash bays to bathe the animals. Each individual stable had its own supply of square bales of straw and hay. All had a handcrafted feed box. Rubs used sat on shelves on the wall. A stable bag with needed harness gear inside, with a personalized logo, hung on a hook outside each large, clean, well-constructed stall that housed the horses. The stable area appeared to be very well cared for. Angel smiled to herself. Stephen had four horses stalled beside her brother's.

Jake walked outside to the trailer. When he returned he hung a harness bag on the hook in front of an empty stall. He turned to face Tim. "*Forever Yours* wears a burr head pole because she likes to bear in on the turns. An open bridle with side rolls so she won't be looking back and lightweight hopples suit her best. Knee and shin boots are worn; she can hit her knees. Also, she tends to kick when she first goes on the track," he informed, patting the horse's muscular neck. "This animal has a lot of talent, but she does have a mind of her own."

Tim unhooked *Forever Yours* from the crossties. "I can handle her," he said, smiling. He walked the horse into the stall, on a fresh bed of straw, added a flake of hay and clean water.

Angel shifted her position on the trunk looking at the three young men. Stephen glanced in her direction. She sighed, rising to her feet. She walked out the entrance, past the jog bikes and sulkies upright outside against the barn wall. She opened the passenger door of the truck and grabbed her knapsack off the seat.

Jake followed. He pulled the heavy ramp up, closed the thin metal top doors, and then put the locks in place. "Get in sis," he said, walking to the driver's seat. He sat and buckled himself in. "Come on, Angel, let's go."

"No. I want to stay here," she said, closing the passenger door.

"Come on, get in the truck!"

"I'm staying with Tim."

"Don't be foolish. You can't stay here. Mom and Dad would freak if I leave without you. Please, get in the truck!"

Angel hadn't considered how her decision would affect others. Even though her choice weighed heavily on her brother, she refused to back down. "I'm not leaving," she said, crossing her arms across her chest. She looked toward Stephen just inside the barn entrance. He stared at her with a slight grin.

Tim stuck his head out of the barn window. "It's okay, Jake, she can stay a few extra days. I'll send her home on the bus," he said, intervening.

"Alright, she's all yours," he said, waving to him out the truck window.

Angel ran around the front of the pick-up truck. She reached in through the window and hugged her brother tight. "Thank you, Jake. Don't worry, I'll be fine," she said, excited.

Jake drove the truck and trailer by the guard shack and then out the long drive.

"See you later, Angel," Stephen said with his thick French accent, walking by her. He sauntered to a grey stone-block building to where he got in the driver's seat of his white truck, revved the engine, and wheeled out of the horse track grounds.

Angel walked to Tim. She smiled to herself, believing she was where she belonged.

CHAPTER THREE

"**H**OME SWEET HOME," TIM laughed opening the tack room door. He stepped inside. Angel followed him through the entrance and looked around. Two light portable beds covered with cotton sheets supplied by their mother, were on either side of the crammed and cluttered room. A small fridge, a three-drawer dresser, a twelve-inch television set, lamp, radio, and hot plate to cook on. Along the back of the grey cement block walls, on nails high hung both oval and round loop-hopples, a few colourful stable halters, as well as a race-harness. Tim's dirty laundry lay piled in one corner. The area looked as if it hadn't been dusted or swept for a month. She wasn't crazy about her new living arrangements. Even though the space was about the same size as her bedroom, the room was quite different than the canopy bed and matching cherry wood furniture she left back home.

Tim laid on a cot putting the pillow under his head, his attention drawn to the game show, *Wheel of Fortune*, that played on the television screen. "Make yourself comfortable, Angel, not much happens here on dark nights," he said, yawning.

Angel closed the door behind her. She tossed her knapsack beside the empty cot, walking toward the refrigerator. "Want something to eat, Tim? She asked.

"No, I'm good, thanks."

Angel opened the refrigerator and retrieved a package of lunch meat, butter and mustard. She removed the twist tie from the bread bag, took out a couple of slices, and then made herself a sandwich. She put the condiments into the refrigerator, and grabbed a few take-out napkins before sitting on the cot.

"How long do you plan to stay?" Tim asked, looking at her.

"As long as you do," she answered with confidence.

"Really! How are you going to support yourself?"

"I can probably find a stable hand job. So, what do you do for fun?" she asked between bites.

"Race horses," he said, laughing.

Angel bent and picked up a photo album from the floor. She put her feet on the cot, her back to the wall, and rested the book on her lap. She thumbed through the pages. Her heart stopped and her eyes widened. Unprepared, she tried to make sense of what she saw. Slowly, she ran her open palm over the plastic protective cover on the picture. Stephen had a gorgeous smile standing beside a horse in the winner circle. He held hands with a pretty, dark-skinned girl the same as him, wearing a stylish mauve dress that did wonders for her youthful body.

"Tim, who's the girl beside Stephen?" she said, trying to sound calm.

Tim looked at her, "Let me see," he said. She flipped the photo album to show him the picture.

"Oh, that's his girlfriend. I can't think of her name. They've been together for as long as I have known him." Unconcerned, he looked at the television screen.

Angel sat in stunned silence, staring at the couple. She never wanted a boyfriend, but now it became a huge deal to make Stephen hers. She wasn't prepared to accept reality. Even faced with the truth, she relied on her romantic fantasy. She shifted and settled in the cot, staring at the game show playing on the television screen. Over and over she replayed seeing Stephen. She didn't have a plan on how to know him better but she believed somehow she would sort things out.

CHAPTER FOUR

THE NEXT DAY ANGEL used her energy cleaning her living quarters. Tim supplied her with a broom, dust pan, clean cloths and a pail of hot, soapy water before leaving to exercise his horses.

She gathered her brother's dirty clothes and put them in a garbage bag to be washed, and then wiped the television set, windowsill and door. She swept the cement floor around the two cots and small dresser. Once in a while she looked outside the tack room to see what was happening. Trainers and grooms who cared for the race horses in their stables consumed the back stretch. She worked without involvement by strangers who mostly spoke French.

Tim entered the tack room. "Wow! Amazing what a little elbow grease can do," he remarked, smiling.

Angel smiled, satisfied with her efforts. "Where can I shower?" she asked, blowing a few strands of hair from her face.

Tim opened the bottom dresser drawer and pulled a folded beach towel, throwing it at his sister. "Come on, I'll show you where the showers are," he said, walking out the open door.

Angel rolled her clean track pants, underwear, and a black spaghetti-strap summer shirt inside the towel with both the soap and shampoo she found on the dresser. She slammed the door shut and raced to catch her brother. The two walked side-by-side close to the edge of a dirt road between the even rows of barns. Horses harnessed, or finishing their daily exercise, jogged on the dirt road that looped around the backstretch.

Approaching a grey brick building, Angel smelled fried food. "The cafeteria is in the back," Tim said as she followed him along the walk outlined with an ankle-height white fence that led toward the entrance. Tim opened the door and they both walked inside.

"I need to enter the horse for the weekend," her brother said, standing to the left in the doorway marked Race Office. "You'll find what you are looking for in there," he said, pointing directly across the hall to the bathrooms labelled male or female.

"Thanks, see you back at the room," she said. The two parted ways. She pushed the door open and stepped inside.

The army green walls and grey cement floor made the cramped space appear dark and dingy. *Definitely not designed to make you feel the comfort of home.* Angel thought wrinkling her nose, as she glanced at the water, toothpaste and hand soap splattered on the long wall mirror over the double sinks, passing the two enclosed toilets. She closed the thin wood door in the small change room and latched the lock. Stripped down to her skin, she turned the water taps on, stepped in and shut the shower door. Steam billowed upward as she stood under the spray washing away the sweat and grime. Pleased that she smelled more of Irish Spring and VO5, Angel shut the taps off, stepped out and dried herself. She tossed on her summer shirt and then stepped into her sweat pants, pushing the material on her legs just under her tanned knees. She rolled her dirty clothes, soap and shampoo in the wet towel. Leaving the washroom she headed straight to her living quarters.

Angel, her hair dripping down her back and shoulders, froze, standing in the doorway as she approached.

"Moving around the furniture definitely made better use of the space, Angel," Stephen commented, the sound of his thick French accent causing her heart to do cartwheels as she watched him stretched on her cot, his back against the wall.

Angel stood, her eyes wide, staring as if in shock.

"Come on in, Stephen brought lunch," Tim said, chomping on a hamburger. Stephen extended a hand that held a paper bag from McDonald's.

"Thanks," she managed with a faint smile, walking in to accept the meal. She sat beside her brother on the edge of his cot and then opened the paper bag on her lap. She dropped her head trying not to stare at Stephen, nibbling on a few French fries. The desire for him that coursed through her excited her within. Her mind raced. She had hope, then nagging doubts crept in. The right side of her brain, the intuitive side, said, once Stephen found time to know her their relationship would grow, but the left side, the logical, argued *what if I'm wrong?*

Angel looked at him, enchanted by his bright ice-blue eyes, resting on her bare tanned legs that stuck out from beneath her rolled track pants. Slowly, he shifted his gaze to her small curves and up to her face and lingered there for a moment. "Are you paddocking *Forever Yours* tonight, Angel?" he asked.

She gave him a warm smile, nodding yes.

"Angel's a good girl," Tim interrupted, "she'll give me a hand, won't you?" he asked, elbowing his sister in jest. "That's why I kept her here, to do my dirty work."

Stephen smiled glancing at his watch. "I've got to go," he said, standing. "I might be back later, but I'm not sure. *Forever Yours* is in the eight race, Tim?"

"Yep, long night ahead," he sighed.

"Is your horse good to go?" Stephen asked, rubbing his hands together.

"If all goes well she should be in the money. She has a good post position."

"Great," he answered, before walking out the door with a slight backwards glance in

Angel's direction.

Angel lay on her cot smiling from ear to ear. Stephen was what made her happy. His tan skin, his curly black hair, intense eyes, lively smile and unique voice.

She slept, her head in her arms, until Tim woke her to harness the horse.

"*Forever Yours* needs to be ready to warm up after the first then run a quick mile after the fifth race," Tim said, walking the horse from her stall, snapping the animal to the crossties. He unzipped the harness bag and removed the race gear. Angel briskly moved a large wooden-handle and a jelly scrubber body brush over and around the animal's muscular frame. She ran a rake comb through *Forever Yours'* mane and tail. She took her time braiding blue and white ribbons; her brother's stable colours, into the horse's lush, long hair on the head and neck. Tim placed a clean cloth onto the cropper and then slipped the gear over the horse's long tail, pulled the harness into place, buckling the belt loosely around her girth. The rich blue fleece back pad matched the coloured fuzzy material Velcroed over the buxton martingale that he snapped onto the harness. With ease he slipped the rubber bell boots over the horse's front hooves. His fingers fumbled with hopple hangers as he hung them in their proper place.

"Feeling good girl," he said to his horse, lifting her front leg and dropped it inside the hopple. The horse lifted the other three legs off the black mat with a gentle touch from his hand.

"You should win for fun," Tim said, giving the horse a loving slap on her neck. *Forever Yours'* ears perked. "She's sharp tonight, sis, we should do well," he said, smiling.

Tim removed the stable halter from the horse's head, replacing the equipment with a double ring-head halter and blind bridle, and then tied the tongue. "Hang on to her, Angel, while I strap on the bike."

Angel held on to the race-halter, leading the horse out of the barn. She stood and looked around. The hustle and bustle in the backstretch on race night was quite different from the deserted area in the afternoon and on dark nights.

"Would you feed supper to mine and Stephen's horses?" Tim asked, tightening the straps to the race bike.

"Sure," she answered, shrugging.

"Stephen's feed is in those small white pails by his stall doors," he said, jumping on the seat. Angel reached for the over check and pulled *Forever Yours* head in place, snapping the clip to the metal ring on the harness. "Meet me in the paddock. We have the two hole. And bring a wash pail with you, please," Tim said over his shoulder, steering the horse away from her.

"Okay," she said, walking to the barn entrance.

Angel advanced to her brother's wood feed box. She mixed the vitamins, grains and sweet feed in four small pails and emptied the feed left for Stephen's horses into the tubs on the wall in their stalls. She tossed each a flake of hay, and then topped the water buckets with the hose. She then put a big sponge, horse shampoo, a scraper and lead chain into a large blue pail. With a cooler-blanket over her arm and the blue pail in her hand she passed horses left and right to meet her brother.

Angel entered the paddock, ignoring the eyes on her. She draped the cooler-blanket over *Forever Yours* steamy, sweaty body and left the ties undone at the neck. She stayed close to the horse and took in surroundings. Horses, one by one, prepared to race, filled the stalls. Whistles could be heard as grooms tried to coax their horse to empty their bladders before each raced. Trainers met with drivers to discuss their race tactics. Owners, dressed in their best, stood looking important.

"Get her ready, sis," Tim said when he returned wearing his blue and white custom racing colours. Angel removed the stable halter from *Forever Yours'* head, replacing the gear with the double ring-head halter and blind bridle, and then tied the tongue. She attached the reins to the bridle as her brother pulled the cooler-blanket off the horse, and then tightened the belt around the animal's girth. Tim attached the light-weight sulky to either side of the horse. Holding the reins he sat close behind the horse. Angel guided the horse out of the crowded paddock and on to the race track.

Angel waited by the high white plank fence while Tim steered *Forever Yours* on her second mile. Bright yellow lights from lamp posts lit the backstretch and the race track. She stared at the brilliantly lit grandstand and wondered if Stephen stood there. Her mind spun with questions. Did he think of her as much as she did of him? Did he want to know her as much as she wanted to know him? Had he fallen for her like she had fallen for him?

"She felt real good during the warm-up, Angel," Tim said, driving his horse off the track, easing her to a stroll.

In the paddock Angel removed the bridle, loosened the harness, gave the animal a light sponge bath, tossed on the cooler-blanket and walked the horse to empty its bladder.

The time slowly passed as she waited for the horse to race. Finally, a loud crackle of the microphone came over the loudspeaker. "Thirteen minutes to post of the eighth race," the announcer said.

Tim used both hands to tighten the belt around *Forever Yours'* girth. He strapped the sulky onto either side of the harness. He gave the horse a quick pat on her neck adding the close bridle to the horse's head. The announcer called the horses on the track for the upcoming eighth race. Tim led the horse out of the building behind the number one horse. His reins man hopped onto the seat of the race bike. Angel followed. Again, a loud crackle came over the loudspeaker, "Introducing your field for the eighth race," the voice boomed.

Angel stood close to Tim watching the post parade. She shook as a cold shiver ran along her spine. Two boys a little older than her, one with dirty blonde hair and husky build, the other a red head, and skinny as a rail, looked at her in a way which disturbed her.

"Starter calls the field to the gate," a loud voice said over the loudspeaker.

The green starter car in front of the grandstand began to move forward. "Field is in the hands of the starter, it's post time." The white gate folded against the side of the car that quickly moved to the side of the track. "They're off!" A roar rose from the crowd.

The horses raced by Angel once, then twice. "The field of horses did their best to keep up, but the final stride belonged to *Forever Yours*, the voice over the loudspeaker announced.

Angel jumped with excitement. Tim's horse did what she was trained to do. Effort paid off, and, as a result, *Forever Yours* finished first. She won in 1:56.

"Come on, sis," Tim said, standing beside a small grey van with the door open. Angel ran to the vehicle climbing in, so happy for her brother she could barely sit still. The driver drove the van on the race track stopping in front of the brightly lit grandstand. Tim slid the door open as the vehicle slowed to a halt. He and Angel jumped out from the back seat. Angel hurried toward the horseshoe-shaped winners' circle. Tim guided *Forever Yours* inside. The reins man dismounted and stood beside the race bike. Angel moved closer to him facing the camera man, searching the crowded grandstand for Stephen. The camera man took the shot blinding her. *Forever Yours'* driver hopped on the seat of the race bike and then steered the tired horse toward the paddock area.

* * * * *

ENTHUSIASTICALLY, TIM RECALLED THE race won to Angel as the van sped on the stone dust covering the racetrack. The driver drove through an open gate and then stopped. Angel hopped out from the van behind her brother. Tim took the driving lines out of the reins man's grip, steering the horse toward the test barn behind the paddock building.

Angel collected the wash pail and cooler-blanket. She entered the test barn. *Forever Yours*, sweaty, stood in the wash stall stripped of her race gear, snapped to the crossties. Angel kept arm's length away holding a large soapy sponge in her hand, washing the large animal. After she rinsed the horse with the hose she scraped the excess water from the animal's brown coat, threw the cooler-blanket on the horse's back, and the lead-chain over the nose, snapping the clip to the stable halter.

Tim approached Angel. The vet followed holding a long yellow stick with a plastic cup attached at the end. The vet paid no attention to her, retrieving the horse's urine sample to be tested for enhancements.

The horse that won the ninth race, breathing heavy through its nostrils and tail twitching, entered the test barn.

"Let's go, Angel," Tim said, throwing the harness gear over his shoulder. He grabbed the wash pail with the supplies inside with his free hand. Angel walked behind him to the stable controlling *Forever Yours* with the lead chain snapped over the nose.

Under the street lamps which lit the dark night, grooms, owners and trainers cared for their horses. Angel stayed close to the barn walking *Forever Yours* to cool the animal's system down. She stopped every few minutes to offer the horse a drink of water. Tim cleaned the harness as strangers to her, but friends to her brother, congratulated him on his victory.

"Bring her in the barn, Angel," Tim said, standing in the warm yellow light at the barn entrance.

Angel put the horse into her stall on a fresh bed of straw. Tim hung the water tub on the wall, tossed in a flake of hay and then fed *Forever Yours* a huge carrot, thanking her for a race well won.

Finished for the night, Angel followed her brother into their tack room, closing the door behind them. Exhausted, she slipped off her shoes, lay on the bed and fell into a deep sleep. Unknown to her, her appearance in the paddock had attracted all kinds of prospects.

CHAPTER FIVE

Aᴺɢᴇʟ ᴡᴏᴋᴇ ᴡʜᴇɴ ᴛʜᴇ bright morning sun shone through the glass panes. She scrambled to her feet, threw on a dark blue spaghetti-strap top and jean shorts, then headed to the stables. She stopped dead in her tracks entering the barn. A boy no older than herself had a horse she recognized from Stephen's stable hooked to the crossties. He crouched beside the lower half of the horse's front leg holding a white cotton wrap in place with one hand between the ankle and knee. He carefully rolled a black brace bandage around the leg.

"Who are you?" she demanded.

"Marcus," he replied. *Quirky looking*, she thought, short, slender with long arms, thin hands and feet, brown hair, freckles, and wearing glasses.

"Where's Stephen?" she asked.

Marcus grabbed a white cotton wrap and black brace bandage from the black mat and began to wrap the opposite leg. "Probably at the flower shop," he said, shrugging.

Angel stepped up to *Forever Yours* hanging her head out the box stall over the hardwood door. "Is that where he is now?" she asked, patting the horse.

Marcus glanced at her. He pushed his glasses back up on his nose. "Would you hand me those bandages?" he asked, pointing to the wrap and brace bandage just out of his reach. Angel walked to the brace bandages, picked them up, and passed them to him.

"From the time Stephen was ten years old he worked at his father's flower shop. He owns the race horses, it's me that is in the barn every morning," he said, wrapping the horse's leg.

"Oh," she said, tossing her long brown hair over her shoulders.

Marcus stood, stretching. He walked to the front of the horse in the crossties, unsnapped the animal from the chains, and then led the horse into the box stall, stepped out, and shut, locking the wooden door. He turned to face Angel. "Not much stands in his way. Work takes up most of his time. That's why my sister, Sophie, is angry with him; most of his attention is taken up with career issues."

"Your sister!" she said, eyes wide.

Marcus pushed his glasses up on his nose. "They just moved into a house. Sophie has had every room painted and they bought new furniture. The place looks great," he said.

Shivers coursed through her as her legs wobbled beneath her. By her own will Angel managed to hold herself upright. A voice screamed in her head, *he's taken! He's really taken. This can't be happening* she thought. His relationship with Marcus' sister can't be that serious.

"What about you, Angel, what's your story?" he asked.

"Just here for the summer," she said, attempting to hide her disappointment.

Angel sat on the lid of the tack box, kicking her heels against the wood. Marcus grabbed the black leather handled driver's whip from where it hung on the wall, striking the end in the open air. Angel flinched from the sound.

"I'm going to be the finest reins' man on the race circuit," he boasted. "Unlike Stephen, I don't want to train or own horses. There is too much manual labour involved and too much of one's own money," he said, flipping the whip. "Do you want to go to the grandstand some night? We can make it a date?" he said, staring at her small chest peeking out from her tank top.

Angel rolled her eyes in disgust. She looked out the open window and noticed an older man, broad-faced, balding on top, wearing a black T-shirt, blue jeans and cowboy boots, approach the stable. He stepped in the barn. "My name is Pierre Bouchard. Are you Angel?" he asked with a thick Quebecois French accent.

"Yes," she said, nodding.

Pierre stood looking at her. "I saw you in the paddock last night working along side your brother. I want to hire you to handle a couple of horses. Interested?"

"Sure, when do you want me to start?" she asked, thinking the job offer slid into place like magic.

Pierre turned toward the open window, pointing to the barn across from Tim's. "I'm stabled there. You can start at seven a.m." With that said her new boss left.

Marcus stood looking at her with his hands deep in his front jean pockets. He had a silly grin plastered upon his face.

"Suppose you can get some work done," said a familiar voice from outside.

Angel jumped to her feet. She rushed to the barn door and looked, grinning from ear to ear. Stephen sat in the driver's side of his white truck. His strong hand gripped the steering wheel. She fixed her eyes on his dark sunglasses and lively smile. "Let's move it, Marcus," he called from his truck.

"I'm coming," he said, walking to the feed box.

"Are you settled in, Angel?" Stephen asked.

"I have a job with Pierre Bouchard," she said as excitement rippled through her stomach.

"Angel, would you dump the feed into the tubs and toss in a flake of hay around six?" Marcus asked pushing his glasses up on his nose.

"Sure."

"Let me know when you want to go to the grandstand together. I'll be sure to get the night off," he said, exiting the barn.

She rolled her eyes in disgust, dismissing his romantic overture. He walked to the white truck, opened the passenger door and sat.

Stephen ran his hand over his dark curly hair. "Well, now that you found employment you'll be too busy for anything else," he remarked, smiling. He waved goodbye before he drove off the track grounds.

Angel walked into her tack room. She could see the potential in the present even with the knowledge Stephen had a live-in girlfriend. She lay on the cot, her mind racing. She wanted to compete for him but she didn't know how. She wouldn't want someone to chase him if he was hers. She didn't know how to pursue him without disappointing her brother. Her emotions had the best of her. Her heart told her to fight for him while her mind asked why?

CHAPTER SIX

"**L**ET'S GO, ANGEL!" TIM said, fully dressed, tying the laces on his running shoes. "We need to go."

"Yeah. I'm up," she said, yawning, rolling on to her back, rubbing her tired eyes.

"Now! You don't want to be late on your first day on the job," he said, standing, walking to the door. He turned the knob and left the room.

Angel sat, reached for her brush, and then brushed the hard bristles through her long hair. She moved her legs to the side and sat on the edge of the cot, squirming to remove the dishevelled T-shirt she had slept in. She leaned to the bottom of the cot and retrieved her knapsack from the cement floor. Rooting in the bag she found a dark blue tank top and navy sweat shorts and changed into the clean clothing. After slipping on her Nike running shoes, she stepped out of the tack room. Her stomach growled as she met her brother outside the barn. She admired the night sky giving way to the dawn walking with Tim in silence along the road. The pair crossed the parking lot crowded with new and used trucks and cars.

"Tim, I need to use the bathroom," she said entering the grey block building.

Tim leaned against the wall and waited for her to exit. The two walked into the cafeteria. The mouth-watering aromas of sizzling bacon, eggs and brewed coffee hung in the air. Angel moved along side her brother with the line of people. Her eyes travelled from table to table. Marcus looked at her with a silly grin and winked. She ignored his advances.

"What will it be?" a woman asked in a thick French accent, wearing a white apron around her ample waist, standing behind the counter.

Angel looked at her brother who scratched the back of his head contemplating their choices. "Two fried egg sandwiches on white toast, chocolate milk and a coffee, double cream and sugar," he said stretching his back.

"Make that two coffees," she said, giving her brother a cool look.

"You sure, sis? I don't think you'll like the taste," he said with a puzzled look.

"I want what you're having," she said raising her eyebrows.

"All right, if you really want a coffee."

The cook prepared their sandwiches. The plump lady behind the counter poured hot, black coffee into two take-out cups, added the cream and two teaspoons of sugar, stirred the steaming liquid, and then capped them off with lids. Tim tossed a crumpled ten dollar bill on the counter. The cashier passed him the order and his change. The two walked out of the building leaving the noise of all the people talking behind.

Angel's hair blew in the morning breeze as she took a sip of her coffee. She smiled to herself enjoying the hot liquid.

Tim wolfed down half his fried egg sandwich walking toward his stable. "Have a good day, sis," he said, looking over his shoulders.

"Yeah, you too," she said, veering toward Pierre's stable. She stopped just inside the door. A beautiful black stallion snapped to the front crossties pawed the black rubber mat with its front hoof. A dance tune blared from the radio resting on a hand made shelf. A girl a couple of years older than Angel, about the same height, dressed in a low-cut pink T-shirt, appearing to be two sizes too small, and a snug pair of cut-off jean shorts, stumbled from the empty stall. Her over-sized boobs almost popped out from the top of her tiny T-shirt as she pushed an orange wheelbarrow filled with dirty, wet straw. She set the wheelbarrow down on its legs. "I'm Kerri. You must be Angel. Pierre said you'd be starting today. Have you ever groomed before?"

"Yeah," Angel replied, nodding.

"Good. I'll show you where everything is kept."

Angel sat on the lid of the metal tack box sipping coffee and eating her sandwich while Kerri showed her where she would find all that would be needed. "You have *Danny Boy*, *Township Sugar* and *Ally B* to care for, Angel," she said, pointing to the horses in stalls, all in a row. "You'll find them easy to jog." Kerri turned and resumed her work.

Angel stood, unlatched the lock on *Danny Boy's* stall, slowly led the animal out, and snapped the horse's stable halter to the free set of crossties. She cleaned the manure from the horse's resting quarters, scattered fresh straw, and then scrubbed the water tubs. *Danny Boy* behaved as she prepared the horse for his daily exercise. Outside in the sunshine, she strapped the job bike onto either side of the harness, sat on the seat, and then followed Kerri and the horse she drove up the dirt road and then on to the race track. Kerri jogged ahead. Horses jogged past her, their hooves pounding against the hard surface.

Twenty minutes later Angel drove *Danny Boy* off the race track steering the horse to the barn.

Angel eased into her job. She removed the dirty straw and cleaned the tubs from the *Township* and *Ally B's* stalls. She tossed the harness gear on Township Sugar, strapped on the jog bike, sat on the seat, and then steered the horse up the dirt road and then onto the track for the animal's daily exercise.

The air was dry and humid when she entered the racetrack with her last horse, *Ally B*.

She had one leg in the stirrup and the other dangling above the ground, steering the horse with the lines between her fingers. She waved to her brother as he exited the racetrack. Louder and louder, hooves hammered the ground behind her, the closer a horse came it seemed to give *Ally B* a boost of energy. Picking up speed, the hot breath from the horse breathed on the nape of her neck. Angel caught her breath, her heart quickly beat gripping the reins. She glanced over her shoulder. "What the hell, Marcus!"

Marcus pushed her and the horse she drove forward. She sat straight, both feet in the stirrups, whizzing by horses in a light jog.

He drove his horse closer.

"Marcus, stop!" she exclaimed over her shoulder.

At the top of the stretch he finally tapped on the brakes and backed off his horse. He steered the animal beside her looking as immature as he acted. "Just having some fun, Angel," he said, grinning.

"You ass!" she said, controlling the large animal's speed. "You could have hurt my horse. Ally could have easily made a misstep and gone down," she said, looking at him.

"Ahhh, just havin' some fun," he reiterated with that silly grin.

"Jerk," she yelled as he drove on.

"Not bad driving for a girl," a familiar voice teased. Angel squinted her eyes from the bright sun as Stephen jogged his horse beside her. Her heart melted being up close and in person.

"Thanks," she said softly.

"*Forever Yours* ran a good race. She paced from fifth to first after being five and a half lengths behind," he said, swerving to miss the horse jogging in front of him.

"Yeah, the race finished in one minute and fifty-six and one fifth seconds," she said, looking at her reflection in his dark sunglasses.

"Tim must be happy. He has a money-maker on his hands," Stephen said, grinning.

"Yeah," she said, nodding.

"You like working in Pierre's barn?" he asked rounding the far turn.

"It's good. I care for three horses; Kerri has four."

"You're close enough to your brother, he'll be able to keep a good eye on you. It doesn't take much to find yourself in trouble around here."

"I'm sure I'll be fine."

"I need to go. I'm going to turn and go a mile," he said, laughing a bubbly laugh that warmed her inside.

"Okay," she said, smiling, jogging ahead to leave the racetrack.

In the barn down the shed row many grooms, trainers and owners worked and talked horses. Angel smiled to herself stripping the harness gear from *Ally B* drenched in sweat. The horse stood pawing the black mat, huffing and puffing, while Angel filled a pail with warm soapy water. She led the horse to the wash stall and gave the animal a bath. With a few quick strokes from a silver scraper she removed the excess water from the animal's chestnut coat. She tossed a dry cooler blanket over *Ally B's* damp coat and then walked the horse into the stall, latching the lock.

Angel wiped the jog harness with a soft clean cloth to remove any dirt or dust, stealing a glance or two at Stephen moving about next door. She placed the gear inside the saddlebag she found the equipment in and closed the zipper, content she had cemented a friendship with him.

Angel unlatched the lock, swung the stall door open, entered, seized *Danny Boy* by his head halter, and then walked the horse into the aisle to snap the horse to the crossties. She slid her hand under the cooler-blanket and across the horse's coat. She pulled the moist blanket off the animal and hung it outside to dry in the hot sun.

Danny Boy stood still and silent as she moved the brush over the animal with a quick flick away and up on the dark coat. She gently combed the mane and tail, and then smoothed down the hair with the body brush. To bring out the horse's shine she wiped *Danny Boy* with a towel.

Angel unhooked the horse from the crossties, walked the animal into the stall, exiting, she latched the lock. She took the same care with *Township Sugar* and *Ally B*, putting them away for the day.

Angel glanced out the window and saw the two young men who gave her the creeps, walking by along the dirt road. They stopped. The young man with the plump figure, short neck, thick dark hair and a full face with a wide mouth and nostrils, yelled toward the barn, "Kerri, are you coming to the cafeteria?"

Kerri walked to the window. "Just wait a minute. I'll be right with you, Bobby," she said. "Would you feed the horses lunch?" she asked, facing Angel.

"Sure," Angel replied, putting the brushes used into the tack box.

"Good," Kerri said, leaving the stable.

Angel looked out the window, chuckling. Bobby's friend appeared quite comical in his appearance. A carrot top, tall, very frail and in need of a good meal. He stood with his hands dug deep into his front pockets of his jeans. Bobby seemed restless, moving from foot to foot. Assuming they were shady she vowed to herself to stay as far away from them as possible.

She walked to the feed box, pulled out the small white pails. She mixed the vitamins, grains and sweet feed together, and fed.

As suddenly as her day had begun, it was over. Angel crossed the grass between Pierre's and her brother's barn on her way to her tack room. She waved to Stephen, sitting in his car, window down, motor running.

"Angel!" Marcus called, exiting the barn.

She paused. "What?" she replied, unconcerned by what he had to say.

"Didn't mean to spook you this morning. It won't happen again," he claimed half-heartedly.

"Whatever," she drawled, rolling her eyes.

Stephen gave her a quick wink as Marcus got into the passenger seat. The two then drove away. Happy with the results of her day, Angel entered the tack room to rest.

CHAPTER SEVEN

ANGEL LOOKED AROUND IN the soft moon rays flooding the tack room with light. In the corner farthest from the door, stood a two-seater, white kitchen table. The radio on the surface played a sentimental country tune. Against the grey block stone wall a single bed with a few sheets on the mattress and two big pillows. She stood, paralyzed. Stephen sat on a brown sofa, gesturing for her to come closer. She slowly walked keeping her eyes on him; his dark curly hair, ice-blue eyes and inviting smile. Quivering, she sat with her leg touching his. He leaned over, touched her cheek, and closed his mouth on hers.

A knock on the door jolted her very much awake. She rubbed her eyes. The moonlight filtered through the window stretched out to disappear on the cement floor. "Let us in, we can have some fun, Angel," Bobby said, his knuckles rapping hard on the door.

Frightened, she waited for her brother to speak but he said nothing.

"Open the door, let us in!" he said, knocking.

Angel pulled back the covers, eased out of bed and quietly tiptoed to her brother. Her hand trembled on his shoulder. "Tim, Bobby and his creepy friend are at the door," she whispered, giving him a gentle shove.

"What!" he said, rolling toward her.

"They want me to let them in to play," she whispered, her insides churning.

Tim sat up, grumpy at being woken up. "Get the hell away from the door, Bobby and George, and don't come back!" he growled loudly.

Angel relaxed, walking to her bed. She lay on the cot under a light blanket, her head in her arms. Minutes passed in silence when Tim struck a brief conversation. "I'm glad you're scared, Angel, you should be home safe in your own bed. The horse track is not a good place for a girl, especially one as young as you. All kinds of tricks and illusions take place. Nothing is as it seems and this includes people. Most of the grooms live, work, and play here, with very little interference from the law. You may think this place is safe when, in fact, that is quite the opposite. This place has hidden traps for the gullible. To trust a stranger would be foolish for most will deceive. Many people hide their motives. While you're here focus on what people do and not what they say. People will show you if they are untrustworthy," he said in the darkened room.

"Okay," she said.

"Now, go back to sleep," he ordered, moving under the covers, settling back in.

Angel slept but with one eye open.

CHAPTER EIGHT

ANGEL LAY ON HER cot wearing a V-neck, black T-shirt and cut off jean shorts. Her eyes glued to Wheel of Fortune playing on the television set. The electric fan blew a cool breeze across her from head to toe.

Suddenly the door opened flooding the tack room with brilliant sunlight. She squinted as Stephen entered closing the door behind him. Her eyes followed him walking toward Tim's cot. "Tim isn't here. He's gone with the blacksmith for the afternoon," she said softly.

"That's okay. What a day, whew, it's hot!" he exclaimed, kicking off his shoes. Hot enough for you, Angel?"

"Yeah," she said, nodding.

He plopped on her brother's cot. "It's been a hot summer," he said, sinking on the mattress. "What are you doing?"

Angel, with her elbow bent, rested her head on the palm of her hand. "Not much. I'm watching *Wheel of Fortune*. Tim has me hooked on the game show," she said with heat rushing to her cheeks.

"I heard you had a couple of midnight callers," he said, running his hand through his dark curls.

"Yeah. Tim told Bobby and his creepy red-headed friend to go away."

"Bobby and George hit on every new girl on the track," he said, attempting to stifle a yawn. "How did you meet the two?"

"I haven't. I saw Bobby and George in the paddock the night *Forever Yours* raced. Then, the first day I worked for Pierre, Kerri hooked up with the pair for lunch. That's it. I have never even had a conversation with them. They give me the creeps the way the look at me."

"Bobby and George are more trouble than they are worth," Stephen said, adjusting his body to a more comfortable position.

Angel shook her head in agreement, with a slight grin. She loved the sound of his voice. His French accent sounded as if he sang his words.

"The friendships you form with people on the track could have repercussions. People are here for a number of reasons. Some can be considered untrustworthy. Most have a real interest in horses, worst case is to do harm. Be careful who you trust; some people are corrupt. There are people who will try to take advantage of you. They will try to manipulate or use you," he cautioned, looking at her.

"People are what they are. You can't change that," she sighed.

"People do what they do. There's no rational explanation why. Remember, it's not what people say, Angel, it's about what they do. People will always show you who they are and their intent."

"Don't worry, Stephen. People may think they can manipulate or use me, but no chance," she said, gazing into his warm eyes.

"You won't know the bad people until they do bad to you. Behave yourself," he said, grinning. "I'm sure all will be fine." Stephen looked at his watch. "I'm going to sleep for a couple of hours. Would you wake me around five," he said, stifling a yawn.

"Yeah," she said, smiling.

Stephen closed his eyes and everything else disappeared for him.

Angel lay on her cot with the television on, looking at him while he slept. He had one arm bent at the elbow, resting over his head, the other arm by his side, his head tilted, his mouth open, breathing heavy and rhythmic. He was the most handsome man she had ever seen. Two hours later he still lay sleeping. He looked peaceful and relaxed. She wondered, did he dream of her or them becoming a couple. She believed she would find true love with him even though she didn't know how to communicate her thoughts and feelings.

Stephen opened his eyes and glanced at Angel, dazed. He looked down at his cotton shirt and navy blue knee-high shorts, and then back at her. "What time is it?" he asked, his voice scratchy.

She lifted her head and looked at the digital clock radio. "It's five to five," she said.

Stephen sat, looking sleepy-eyed. "I should go. I have a horse racing in the sixth race tonight," he said.

"Want some help?" she offered.

"No. Marcus is around here somewhere. But thanks for the offer," he said, standing.

"Would you ask Marcus to feed Tim's horses supper for me?" she asked, her eyes following him to the door.

"No problem," he said, leaving, closing the door tight.

Angel rolled onto her back, giggling like the school girl she was. Stephen's visit couldn't have made her happier. So far she had turned her plans into reality. Everything had come together except she knew the man of her dreams wasn't single.

She stayed in the tack room on her cot, staring at the images that flashed across the television screen with the sound turned down. Time had slowly passed when the announcer called Stephen's horse race onto the track. Angel bolted upright, slipped her bare feet into her Nikes, opened the door and stepped outside. The sky had darkened. A bright full moon hung in the star speckled sky, and not a cloud to be seen. The soft light from the street lamps shone down lighting the dirt road as she hurried along, heading straight for the ten feet high white plank wooden fence. She stood and looked between the boards at the horses on the racetrack. Stephen flashed her a smile, jogging by wearing a one piece quilted nylon race suit with gold and black across his chest, back and his short sleeves. He had his initials in black material sewn on a white circle to the upper arm. The yoke had black stars on a gold background. His pants, white with gold and black piping down either leg that matched his stable colours. She thought he looked professional dressed in his custom suit. He appeared as casual as casual could be on the seat of the sulky, feet in the stirrups, the reins in his hands, positioning his horse behind the starting gate, and then they were off. The announcer called Stephen's horse, *Peesu Peesu* on the front. A surge of adrenaline swept through her as a clatter of hooves whizzed past her. Angel stood biting her nails, afraid and excited for Stephen. The sulkies and horses were closely packed together pushing forward. *Peesu Peesu* led down the straightaway and around the far turn. She looked across the grassy infield as the nine horses raced over the finish line in front of the grandstand. The announcer announced Stephen had steered *Peesu Peesu* to a win of 1:55.2. The small van drove by her on the way to the winner's circle with Marcus beaming in the back seat.

Angel couldn't have been happier for Stephen. She wanted to run to the paddock to congratulate him, but, believing he was all business when he raced, she walked with a skip in her step to his stable. She sat on the tack box and waited for him to return from the test barn.

"What are you doing here?" Marcus asked, leading *Peesu Peesu* through the entrance.

"Where's Stephen?"

"Coming," he said, snapping the horse to the crossties. He pulled the damp cooler-blanket off the horse and tossed on a dry one. He peered at Angel from behind his glasses. "Why are you looking for him?"

"I wanted to congratulate him on his win," she said, smiling.

Marcus wasn't impressed. "I do all the work and you're going to praise him. Typical."

"What?" she asked, raising her eyebrows.

Marcus walked into the horse's stall, brought out the water tub and placed the container on the ground just outside the barn door. When he returned he gawked at her in a way that made her uncomfortable. Squirming in her seat, her joy fell away to shock. Her pulse quickened. Stephen walked into the building with his fingers locked around the fingers of the girl in the picture. Sophie appeared more gorgeous in person with her dark curly hair flowing down her shoulders, and perfect figure. Angel bit her trembling lip, looking at every move the couple made together. Stephen released his hand from Sophie's. He walked toward her, grinning. "Did you see *Peesu Peesu* race, Angel? Man, she won for fun," he said, putting his painted helmet on the tack trunk.

"What? Oh, yeah," she stammered, "you had an easy time finishing first."

Sophie glared at her, walking to Stephen. She touched his upper arm. "With you as the reins man, how can one be surprised at the outcome?" she purred.

Angel leaped to her feet. Her knees almost buckled. She crossed the shed row, catching Stephen steal a glance at her. She exited the big sliding doors, passed Marcus cooling down *Peesu Peesu*, heading toward her tack room.

She sat on her cot, her head in her hands. Pressing her palms against her forehead, she tried to erase the image of Stephen and Sophie together. "I'm the one you're supposed to be with, me. I'm the one! Why can't you see this?" she said in an aggressive whisper.

"Hey, Angel," a familiar voice said. She looked up to see Stephen standing inside the doorway. He appeared exhausted after a long day's work, then six hours racing his horse. "Are you okay?" he asked with concern. "You don't look good."

"Yeah, I'm fine, just tired," she replied, shrugging.

"Did I do something?"

"No, I'm really happy for you, really. I'm just tired."

Stephen stood for a moment, his eyes fixed on her. "Okay, then, I'm going to slip off my race suit. Sweet dreams," he said with a wink.

"You, too," she said as heat rushed to her cheeks.

Stephen left, smiling.

Angel lay her head on the pillow. She couldn't shake the sight of Sophie. She hadn't thought there would be a possibility that she would come in contact with her, but she had and now she couldn't rid the image from her mind. The time slowly ticked by as she fell into sleep.

CHAPTER NINE

A<small>NGEL, LOST IN HER</small> thoughts, gently combed *Township's* mane, staring out the open window at Stephen working in the barn next door. The proposition she expected hadn't come even though she knew he had a committed relationship, a house, and two careers. She tried not to allow her disappointments to get the best of her. She valued his friendship. She wanted to express her heart to him, but he was devoted to another.

"You involved with him," Kerri asked.

Angel hesitated. "No, he's a friend," she replied.

"To you or Tim?"

"Both."

"I wouldn't blame you if you have the hots for him. He's a total stud, but don't waste your time. He thinks he's better than us, only 'cause we live on the track and party."

Angel kept her words guarded. "He's not like that. Stephen is a sweet guy."

"He has you fooled. I've seen the way he looks at you, and there are only two types of women in a guy's life, the one he is screwing and the one he wants to screw. Which one are you?"

"Neither," she said softly. "He's a nice guy to spend time with."

"Don't dwell on him, move on," Kerri said, unhooking her horse from the crossties, setting the horse free to run into the stall. "Maybe you and Stephen are not built to go the distance. If he wanted to be with you, he would. It may be time to put yourself back out there."

"Out where?" she said, surprised.

"After the races tonight a bunch of us are going down the road to the Inn for a few drinks. Want to come?"

Swayed by Kerri reinforcing the relationship wouldn't go the way she believed it would, she agreed.

Later that night when the race card was concluded, Kerri, wearing a skin-baring, sultry bustier-style black shirt and tight blue jeans, stood in the doorway of Tim's tack room. She had her nails painted black and her heels matched her purse.

Tim took his eyes off the television screen, checked out Kerri, and then looked at his sister wearing a plain white T-shirt, her favourite jeans and Nikes. "Going somewhere,

Angel?" he asked.

"Yeah," she said, smiling sheepishly.

"Where?"

She cleared her throat. "Out with Kerri."

"Yes, I can see that, but where?"

"Let her come with me, Tim," Kerri said, interrupting. "We are only going dancing down the road at the Inn."

"Please," Angel begged.

"Fine, but be careful," he cautioned in an authoritative voice.

"I will, Tim, I promise," Angel promised over her shoulder, walking out the door. She followed Kerri across the grass between barns, jumped into the passenger seat of the beat up pick-up truck. She admired the pink, fuzzy dice that hung from the rear view mirror. Kerri turned the key in the ignition, the motor roared after two tries. She drove past the guard shack with the music blaring through the speakers. At the end of the long lane she quickly looked both ways for oncoming traffic, and then squealed the tires around the corner and on to the main road. Minutes later she wheeled into the Inn's parking lot and found a spot to park.

"Let's go!" she said, stepping out of the truck. Angel opened the door and climbed out. She followed close behind her new friend, not knowing what to expect, but with all work and no play, she was up to just about anything. She walked between the parked cars to the wood steps of an older timber frame building. A strong beat surged through the open doors as they entered. Angel trailed Kerri who pushed through the crowd heading straight for the bar.

"What will it be, Kerri?" the bartender said, staring at her enormous chest she displayed so proudly.

"Vodka and orange for me," she cooed. "What about you, Angel?"

Quickly she thought, she liked ginger ale and her uncle always drank gin, "Gin and ginger ale, please," she said.

"Strong drink for a little girl," the bartender smirked, pouring their beverages. Kerri bought. Angel drank some of her drink enjoying the taste. She bought the second round. She sat on a stool at the bar moving her body with the beat of the dance tune the DJ spun. Kerri worked the room, hugging everyone she met.

Angel looked around the dimly lit area for Stephen. Men and women, some she recognized from the horse track, moved about or sat at the saloon-style tables and drank.

The people on the dance floor flailed their arms and legs to the strong beat. But, in the crowd, Stephen could not be found.

Bobby and George stood close by with a beer in their hands. She met with Bobby's eyes, shivering as a cold chill ran along her spine. He looked at her as if he wanted to devour her like an animal who hadn't eaten in days.

"Come on, Angel!" Kerri said, as she grabbed her by the arm, leading her toward the dance floor.

"No, I don't think I can," she stammered, following against her will.

"Yes you can. Allow yourself to feel the music, just let yourself go!" she said, stretching her arms wide, twirling on the dance floor. Her feet, hips, arms and head moved to the beat. Angel mimicked Kerri's moves at first, and then eagerly danced along to the tune the DJ played. She drank, danced, and became better acquainted with her new friend until the bar closed. Drenched in perspiration, she slipped through the crowd and out to the parking lot. Intoxicated, she stumbled into the passenger seat, buckling herself in. Kerri turned on the ignition key. The old truck roared, and then settled down. Headed to the race track, she drove fast. "Bobby's fixed on you," she said, taking her eyes off the road.

"I thought he was interested in you. Earlier, at the bar, I saw his arm tight around your waist," she slurred.

Kerri rolled her window down, breathing in some air. "He wants to hook up with you. He's more suitable for you than Stephen. Bobby's perfect," she said, smiling.

"That's a joke, right? Bobby's a jerk. I love Stephen."

Angel shook her head in disbelief. She couldn't believe what she had said. She had tried to keep her desire for him under wraps, but the alcohol she drank helped loosen her lips. Her feelings for him were out in the open.

Kerri wheeled the truck down the long laneway. "Love is for fools," she smirked. "No one falls in love. People hook up 'cause they are into each other at that moment—they are in lust."

She stopped the truck at the guard shack and showed her ORC to the guard. "Your relationship with Stephen isn't a fair one," she said driving through the open gate. "He comes and goes, leaving you here alone. It's not a fair trade off. Don't you think you deserve more? If he really wanted you he'd be here for you and he's not," she said, driving the truck along the dirt road. "You don't need to chase anyone only to be snubbed. Stephen hasn't taken any notice of you, has he, where Bobby has."

Kerri turned the ignition off, opened the door and stepped out in front of her tack room. "See ya tomorrow," she said, slamming the door closed.

Angel fell out of the passenger seat onto the cool ground.

Alone under the starry night sky, she stumbled to her tack room. She made it to the door, turned the handle and struggled inside. Tim slept as she fell onto her cot. Even though the room spun, she closed her eyes and fell asleep while images of Stephen danced in her head.

CHAPTER TEN

THE SUMMER NIGHTS OF August were filled with parties. Angel and Kerri continued to close the bars. A typical night for the two were a few shots of sambooca, lit on fire and two or three of their favourite alcoholic beverages. Angel would wake each morning on the verge of dying. Her head and body ached and any moment she'd throw up.

One sunny afternoon shortly after she fed Pierre's horses lunch, Stephen pulled up to his barn in his white truck. "Are you going to talk to him, Angel?" Kerri asked, standing at the barn door.

Angel glanced out the window at him wearing a black T-shirt and boot cut jeans, enter his stable. "No. I've been avoiding him for the past few weeks. I can't chase someone who doesn't want me," she said, even though her heart continued to pull her in the opposite direction.

"Good decision. I'll see you tomorrow." Kerri left, heading toward her aged pick-up truck.

Angel, with her head hung low, crossed between the two barns and then into her tack room. Tired and ill, she fell onto her cot and closed her eyes. Minutes later, startled, she scrambled to sit when Stephen charged into the room. "What are you doing?" he said, voice rising.

"I was laying, listening to the television. Why?"

"Don't be smart! You drink steady, closing the bars. You are around the wrong people."

Angel remained cool and collected despite the fact she wanted to throw up. "Kerri's alright, she just likes to go to the bar and have fun."

"Kerri is a hot mess. She has a drinking problem. The longer you hang with her, you, too, could become a drunk."

"What?" she said, surprised. "Kerri's not a drunk, she likes to go to the bar to unwind after work."

"You two are out four or five nights a week, drinking," he said, shaking his head in disbelief.

"What's wrong with having a few drinks? I'm not a child. I can do what I want, when I want. I can, and will, make my own decisions," she challenged.

"You can't stay sober with Kerri."

"Who says I want to, and Kerri isn't a bad influence. She's my friend. We're tight."

Stephen walked to her cot and sat, looking at the grey cement floor.

"Don't worry, Stephen. I'm okay. Honest," Angel reassured him, brushing the long bangs from her eyes.

"Angel, I don't know you any more. It's almost as if parts of you have disappeared since you met her. You're a good girl and you're becoming like her."

"Stop, Stephen! Kerri has been a friend to me."

"You know what Bobby wants from you. Why would you put yourself out there to be hurt?" he said, running his hand over his black curls.

"Hurt?" she said, eyebrows raised. She grabbed his shoulders and jerked him toward her. She angled her head and kissed him hard on his soft lips. Stephen pulled away, meeting her eyes. He ran his fingers lightly across her cheek. His head slanted he put his lips over hers, kissing her long and passionately. Angel, lost to the moment, drew him closer. Her heart boomed as her body feverishly quaked. He shifted, circling his arms around her, and cuddled her close, burying his face in her hair. She sighed, settling her head against his shoulder, breathing in his intoxicating cologne.

Stephen's embrace stiffened. He pulled away. "Sorry. I need to leave," he said, standing.

Angel sat shell-shocked. She could read in his eyes regret and it worried her. "Okay," she said softly.

He stepped back, turned and left the tack room.

A part of her heart ripped when he closed the truck door and drove away.

CHAPTER ELEVEN

"**Y**OU NEED TO START packing. We leave in three days," Tim said, stepping into the tack room.

Angel's whole body jolted awake. Her head spun from the alcoholic drinks she had consumed the night before. Blurry-eyed, she looked at her brother. "Don't joke," she said, rolling on to her side.

Tim kicked off his shoes. He turned on the television set and switched channels until he found the station playing *Wheel of Fortune*. He flopped on his cot, grabbed the pillow, and put it under his head. "No joke, sis, we are going home Monday. My horses need a rest and you need to go back to school," he said.

Angel sat and rubbed the sleep from her eyes trying to comprehend what her brother said. *Go home*, she thought, *I don't want to go home*. She rocked back and forth while her mind raced for a solution. Her thoughts jumped from one idea to another. She had a difficult decision to make between right and wrong. Her desire for Stephen, and her obligation and duty to her family. Her thoughts were split. One was what she wanted to do, the other was what she ought to do. She knew she shouldn't stay and pursue Stephen. He was taken, but to go would leave her empty. She had hoped for her and Stephen since the kiss they shared. Even though she rarely saw him. He came early, dropped off Marcus, only to return after two p.m. for his groom, and then gone again.

"I'm not going home, Tim," she said, looking at him.

Tim pushed up on his elbow, half turned, his eyes met with hers. "Really," he said.

"I can take care of myself. I'll work hard over the winter, save some money and buy a horse to train," she said, staring at him.

"That's the craziest idea you have ever had," he said, laughing. "School starts after Labour Day, and, guess what, sis, that's where you'll be. It's the end of your bad behaviour."

"I can take care of myself," she simply stated. "I'm independent. I make my own money."

"I'm done listening to your endless banter. I've said all I'm going to say. We're leaving Monday!"

Angel spent the next three nights tossing and turning. The move preoccupied her mind. Moody and withdrawn she couldn't accept her time at the horse track was over. On the day of the move she tossed her clothes into her school knapsack while her brother carried a load of race gear to his truck. *Who does Tim think he is, he's not my father*, she thought. *I don't have to take orders from him*. She walked out the tack room door and, instead of turning left toward the truck and trailer, she turned right. She followed the dirt road along the back of the long Indian red barn. She rounded the corner and checked for her brother. Seeing him nowhere in sight, she crossed the grass between the barns, through the sliding doors, and quickly crept up the shed row to Pierre's stable. She unlatched *Township Sugar's* lock on the stall, opened the door enough to slide in, and then pushed the latch closed. She crouched against the wall in the corner upon the clean straw. The horse munched on the hay beside her. Her mind drifted along with music that belted out from the radio on the shelf.

Tim loaded the last of the bags. He quickly became annoyed talking to grooms, trainers, and owners, looking for her. He widened his search. His attempt brought him no luck. Angel stayed hidden afraid he'd find her, then again, that he wouldn't. Tim checked and re-checked the back stretch. By late afternoon he turned the key in his truck's ignition. Minutes later he was gone. Angel stood, stretched and then picked up her knapsack. She thought about what she had done. Her brother had protected her and now she was on her own, flying solo. She may have seen herself as independent, but she suffered.

Angel exited the stall. She fed Pierre's horses supper. She leaned toward the open window as a hum of motor crawled along the dirt road. Stephen's white pick-up truck emerged and parked. He pulled the keys, opened the door, stepped out, slamming the door shut. She tried to steady herself from trembling, crossing between the two barns. She entered his stable. "Hi, Stephen," she said, standing in the entrance.

Startled, he turned to face her. "What the hell are you trying to pull? Your brother is worried. You need to call home."

"I'm not going home. I want to taste life and experience things I've never experienced," she said sternly, walking to him. She left out that she planned to follow her heart and pursue him.

He looked at her with a curious smile. "Life here is full of experiences, exposure, and swift transitions, some good, some bad. I don't know if you're old enough to handle what's to come, Angel."

She smiled. She loved the way his words rolled off his tongue. No matter what he said the words sounded like poetry.

Stephen sat on the lid of his tack box. "You're an independent little thing," he said, laughing, shaking his head. "Where do you plan to stay?"

"I don't know. I hadn't thought about that," she said, standing closer to him.

"I should send you home." His eyes met hers. "Come with me," he said, standing. He walked across the shed row, and out the sliding door. Angel followed close beside him not knowing what to expect. He opened the door to the tack room beside what was her brother's. She walked in behind him. The tiny room looked like the one in her dream. In the corner furthest from the door stood a white kitchen table with two chairs. A radio sat on the surface. Against the grey stone-block wall a single bed with a few sheets on the mattress and two big pillows and directly across, a worn brown couch. Beside the door sat a fridge with a television set on top.

"I'm supposed to send you home on the bus, that is if I was lucky enough to find you. At least in here I can keep an eye on you," he said, smiling.

Stephen stood in the doorway. "I gotta go. Make yourself comfortable and, whatever you do, lock the door before you sleep," he said with a wink.

Angel turned the television set on. She lay stretched on the single bed. She couldn't be happier. Her situation couldn't have turned out much better.

CHAPTER TWELVE

WORK OCCUPIED MOST OF Angel's time. She rose at five-thirty in the morning and fed Pierre and Stephen's stables. She spent seven hours during the day exercising and the care of Pierre's horses assigned to her, another six hours paddocking on race nights, and, on Saturdays, usually with a terrible hangover, she'd rush to be done before the schoolers, qualifiers, or the full race card began. Nothing made her happier than the afternoons, few and far between, that she and Stephen spent in peaceful conversation. However, they never took the time to discuss expanding their relationship. She became scattered taking advantage of the lack of supervision. Angel wanted excitement and happiness.

On this night she sat squashed in the cab of Kerri's truck between her and Bobby. Angel squirmed in her seat, faced forward, mesmerized by the headlights of the oncoming traffic while Kerri and Bobby bickered.

"Screw you, Bobby! Your horse parked mine," Kerri said, driving off the track grounds. "My horse was stuck against the rail and yours on the outside, one horse in front and the rest of the field behind."

Bobby looked past Angel and spoke. "Your horse had the two hole, mine the four. Your driver had a better chance to move up the rail for a good position. Instead, my horse gets stuck on the outside and lost ground on every turn."

"For real, Bobby. My horse was stuck parked in the pocket by yours on the outside," Kerri smirked, wheeling her truck into the Inn's parking lot, sliding to a stop. A cold blast of wind blew through the cab when she opened the door and stepped onto the pavement. Angel slid across the seat and hopped out from the passenger side behind Bobby. The frosty air brushed against her skin. She broke from her trance looking from the snow-covered pavement. Marcus, dressed in western shirt, his winter coat and jeans, stood waiting for Stephen to exit his truck. Angel hesitated, and then continued to walk toward the wood building, smiling to herself. Inside, she followed Kerri and Bobby heading for the bar. Stephen and Marcus walked to the saloon-style tables and chairs.

The bartender leaned across the bar. "Gin and ginger, Angel?" he asked, smiling.

"Yep," she said, reaching into her jean pocket and pulled a crumpled five dollar bill, tossing the money on the bar. Angel gripped her glass, stirring her drink with the swizzle stick. She glanced at Stephen wearing a soft black leather jacket over a dark blue sweat shirt, then away sipping her drink.

"Give it up already. You don't need him. Can't you see he doesn't want you!" Kerri shouted over the blaring music.

"He's good to me. He listens to my problems when I'm having a bad day. He'll drive me to the store when I need something. He took me to Kmart to buy this winter coat. He's my friend, but some day he will be my boyfriend," Angel insisted.

Kerri waved to the bartender for a drink. "Are you kidding, Angel? Stephen doesn't give a damn about you. He has a life off the track that includes a live-in girlfriend. Nothing you do will change that. He'll stop by your tack room and then he won't show again for days. You must be lonely. You've been without someone for so long. Stop trying to please him and move on."

Angel stirred her drink, thinking. She hoped sooner or later he would fall in love with her and split from Sophie. Even though she didn't want to hear what Kerri had to say, Angel knew she spoke the truth. Stephen was only a few feet away, yet he hadn't come to say hi.

Kerri tossed her long blonde hair around her shoulders. "If he wanted to be with you he would. You either feel it or you don't. Stephen doesn't feel for you. Quit pining for him. Now, on the other hand, Bobby is ready, willing and able to be with you," she reasoned.

"No!" she said abruptly. "I don't want Bobby."

"Okay then, to get what you want from Stephen play the game, dance with Bobby. If he cares, he'll become jealous and react. But I wouldn't expect much from him."

Angel looked at Bobby drinking his beer. Tempted, she took a deep breath and exhaled. Bobby pushed Kerri to the side. "Kerri's right, you should dance with me, Angel," he said, spraying his words at her.

He grabbed her hand trying to bring her to the dance floor. She dug in her heels shaking his grip free. "Let go of me!" she growled.

Kerri smiled an absolutely wicked smile. "Forget it, Bobby. Come with me, Angel," she shouted over the throbbing, thumping music.

Angel stumbled as she was being dragged to the dance floor. She caught Stephen's eyes swing onto her. He ran his fingers through his dark curly hair as he had the habit of doing.

"You're hopeless," Kerri said, dancing around her. Angel made an effort to move like her friend, twirling with self-confidence and a certain sex appeal, wearing trashy, stylish, body-enhancing attire.

Angel attempted to distance herself from Bobby, rubbing his sweaty body close to hers. She pushed him away, but he would only crowd her more.

Angel and Kerri drank, laughed and danced to the pulsating music until last call.

"I'm going to the washroom. When I get back we'll leave," Kerri announced over her shoulder.

Angel stood at the bar and waited for her to return, letting her eyes adjust from the dimness to the sharp light. She turned at the soft tap on her shoulder. She locked eyes on Stephen. He leaned into her ear. "I'll give you a ride back to the track," he whispered.

"Okay," she said without taking her eyes off him.

"She's coming with us," Kerri slurred, looping her arm in Angel's. "We are off to an after hours club."

Stephen gulped his drink and placed the empty glass on the bar. He had a look in his eyes Angel hadn't seen before.

"No, she's not, Kerri. You and Bobby go and enjoy yourselves. Grab your coat, Angel," he commanded in his strong French accent.

Stephen and Marcus walked to the front door. Angel followed, smiling to herself leaving with him. Outside the cold air flew into her lungs. Her Nike shoes crunched across the snow covered parking lot to the white pick-up truck. She climbed into the cab and heaved herself in the middle seat. Marcus slid in beside her. Stephen opened the driver's door, got in and turned on the engine. He waited for a car to pass and, with one hand on the wheel, he pulled onto the main highway. He stared out the windshield, driving. Way ahead he put the turn signal on then braked and aimed for the race track's long laneway. He dropped his window an inch at the guard shack and showed his ID.

"Wait here, Marcus," he said, parking the truck. He removed the keys from the ignition, opened his door, then stepped onto the ground. Angel walked into his moonlit tack room behind him. Stephen closed the door. Angel turned to flick on the light switch.

"Don't," he said, placing his palm on her hand. "Can we just lay together? I'm too tired to drive."

"Sure," she whispered, her heart racing.

Stephen walked to the bed. He slipped out of his black leather jacket, tossed his coat on the couch, kicked off his shoes, and lay with his back against the grey brick-stone wall.

"Is there room for me?" Angel asked, taking a deep breath.

"*Oui,*" he said, on the other side of the room, staring at her.

She walked toward him, tossed her coat on his, sat on the edge of the mattress, and slipped out of her Nikes but kept her socked on as she lay beside him, trembling. Stephen curved his body close to hers in a cozy spoon position and wrapped his arm tightly around her waist. She reached for his hand. Her heart skipped a beat when he didn't pull away. With hers and Stephen's head on the same pillow, she felt his hot breath on the nape of her neck. The excitement and anticipation within, kept sleep at bay as she lay cuddled against his warm body. She wanted him to hold her, to love her.

Angel lay quiet, staring at the soft light from the lamp post that crept through the blinds. She dared not move for fear she'd wake him and he'd leave. She tried to think of ways she could talk about their relationship. Her mind fumbled to put her emotions into words.

"You should go home to your family. The race track is not a good place for a girl to be," he whispered close to her ear.

"Stephen," she interrupted.

"Honestly Angel, real bad things can happen. People you think are your friends will mislead you. You could be disillusioned and disappointed when you discover their true motives."

"I hate to break the news to you, people can be bad," she frowned. "They say bad things, *they* do bad things, they are bad. No one's perfect."

"There needs to be bad people. How else could you appreciate the good people?" he said against her hair.

She shifted her body to face him. "Are you one of the good ones?"

"I like to think so," he said, looking at her with affection. He paused. His eyes drifted from her. "I'm your friend. Always have, always will be—but I can't be more," he said, his eyes filled with hurt.

Angel sat, cross-legged, on the bed. Stephen placed his hand on her thigh. "I like you," he said. "But it's not enough. You're too young. I can be your friend, you can always count on me. I'll always be near if you need someone to talk to."

"You're wrong," she said with panic in her voice. "I'll strive to do good and prove myself to you. Show you I'm worthy enough to be your girlfriend. I'm willing to try. Don't say no, please!"

"You're not old enough."

"Yes, I am. I believe in us. I believe we have a connection."

Stephen sat on the edge of the mattress staring at the cement floor. "I can't. I can't disregard my commitments. Sophie loves me. She's loyal. If I cheat with you, I'll break her heart and you will never trust me. You'll always think of me as one of the bad people in your life. I want to be with you. I do have strong feelings for you." He turned to look at her over his shoulder. "But I can't and I won't. Chalk us up to bad timing. If I were younger or you were older things would be different. Maybe we could give us a go, but it is what it is," he said, touching her cheek with his fingertips.

Angel shook, brushing her long bangs from her eyes. She leaned and placed her lips on his. His mouth took over hers, burying his hands in her long hair. He wrapped his strong arms tightly around her. With her arms around his neck, she hugged him back, nuzzling her face against his shoulder.

"I need to go," he murmured.

Stephen stood up, slipped on his jacket, then walked toward the door. He paused. "Angel." She refused to look at him. "I sold two of my horses. I'm giving Pierre *Toner* to train. I won't be here much. Any time you need to talk I'm a phone call away," he said, concerned.

Angel didn't turn around. She couldn't. Her lip trembled as the tears welled. She'd be a fool she thought if she tried to make him stay so she let him go.

Stephen opened the door, then left. The driver's side door of his white pick-up truck slammed shut moments later. The truck in gear, Stephen tramped on the gas and drove away from the track grounds.

CHAPTER THIRTEEN

Mᴀʀᴄʜ SHOWED ITS BITTER side with a vengeance. Cold winds, ice storms and heavy snow lasted for weeks. April's heavy rains washed away the snow that had accumulated. By May the blizzard and rainy season came to an end.

On a sunny Tuesday afternoon Angel lay on her bed. Bored, she flicked through the channels in search of something, anything, on television. Her tack room door swung open. She lifted her head and stared at Kerri wearing a yellow spaghetti strap shirt and cut-off jean shorts.

"Hey, Angel. Whatcha up to?" she asked.

Angel sat on the mattress. "What do you want?"

Kerri walked across the cement floor. "What are you watching?" she asked, plopping herself on the brown couch.

"Nothing."

"George and Bobby are having a few drinks in their tack room. I've come to get you to join," she said, looking at the television screen.

"No thanks. I'll pass," she said, swatting at the fly that flew through the open door and around her head.

"Ohhh, don't be like that, Angel. Come drink with us."

Angel sighed, contemplating the invitation.

"Just come for one," Kerri begged.

"All right," she said, annoyed.

Angel stood and straightened the dishevelled navy blue summer shirt and gym shorts she wore. She slipped her bare feet into her Nikes and then followed Kerri out the door.

She walked beside her close to the edge of the dirt road between the even rows of horse barns, and entered the tack room that smelled of spilled beer behind Kerri. She looked to George reclined on a worn blue easy chair, his leg flung over the arm cushion. He had a mischievous look in his eye. Bobby lay flat on his unkempt bed wearing summer shorts and socks with a week's worth of grime on the bottom. Kerri climbed onto the mattress, sat next to him, their bodies touching, and settled in.

"Come on in, Angel," Bobby said, looking over his shoulder. He gestured to George for a wine cooler. George reached into the fridge beside him, grabbed a wine cooler, flicked the cap off and handed the bottle to her.

"Thanks. What are you watching, George?" she asked, sitting at the foot of the bed.

"*Nothing to Lose*," he answered with a sideways glance.

"What's the movie about?"

"A would-be robber who tried to car-jack some crazy chick's car."

"Any good?"

"What's with all the questions?" Kerri asked, annoyed.

The room hushed. Angel's attention turned toward the screen. From the corner of her eye she caught Kerri running her fingers through Bobby's thick brown hair. The smile on his face showed he approved.

"Want another, Angel?" George asked after he polished off the wine cooler he held.

"No. I haven't finished the one I have," she said, raising the almost full bottle in the air.

Kerri kissed Bobby's neck, rubbing her hands slowly and seductively over his body. She gave his ass a forceful squeeze, and then bit into a cheek. Bobby groaned as she slipped her hand between his thighs, trailing her tongue along his spine.

George kept his eyes on them with his one hand deep in front jean pocket. Angel took a deep breath looking at the garbage and dirty clothes scattered on the cement floor.

"Don't restrain yourself, Angel, join in," Kerri said, massaging Bobby's skin.

"You want me to feel him, like you!" she said outraged, raising her voice.

"Go ahead, he won't bite," Kerri purred.

"I don't want any part of this!" she said, shifting to the outer edge of the bed. She set the wine cooler she drank from on the floor.

"Don't be such a baby, Angel. We all have needs, and yours haven't been filled for a while," Kerri coaxed, trying to pressure her. She reached over and took Angel's hand laying the palm on Bobby's hairy calf. Angel roughly pulled her hand away, wiping it on her shorts. Suddenly nothing seemed more important than to find a way out. "I don't want any part of your deviant behaviour. There is no way I'm going to sink to your level," Angel stood up to leave.

Kerri laughed at her naïvete. Angel stomped out, slamming the door behind her. She turned left instead of right which would have lead her to her tack room. *What the hell? What the hell?* She thought, heading to the pay phones across from the race office. She slid the plexiglas shut and sat on the metal seat, pausing to examine the quarter she held between her fingertips. "Heads," she whispered, "yes, tails, no." She tossed the quarter into the air. The silver piece rotated upward and then fell. She caught the quarter in mid-air and quickly flipped the coin onto her forearm. She smiled to herself, opening the phone directory. She ran her finger down the page and searched for *his* home number when she changed her mind and thumbed through the yellow pages in the flower shop listings.

Angel's heart raced dropping the quarter in the pay slot. Consumed with anxiety she dialled the number. "The Flower Wagon," a familiar voice said on the other end of the receiver.

"Hey, Stephen. You said it was okay to call," she whispered.

"It is," he said in a bubbly voice. "Is everything okay?"

"Yeah," she sighed.

"I'm glad you called. I've been thinking about you. I'd come and see you, but I've been busy at the store. My dad retired and I'm running the entire show."

"Wow! That's cool."

"Are you sure everything is okay?"

"Well, I'm not friends with Kerri. She has made my life a living hell. I'd quit and find another job, but I love caring for *Toner*." She paused. "Did you know your horse is in Friday night?"

"Yes. I saw him in the entries from the sports section of the newspaper.

"Are you coming to watch him race?"

Stephen hesitated. "I'm not sure. I'll try. I don't want to promise. Things could change between now and then."

"Yeah. You're right," she said, sighing.

"I need to hang up, Angel. A couple just entered. Please, feel free to call again."

"I will."

The phone line went dead.

Angel walked the dirt road to her tack room. The unpleasantness she had experienced with Kerri was behind her. She tingled inside, rekindling her friendship with him.

* * * * *

STEPHEN DIDN'T SHOW UP on Friday night when *Toner* raced, still, he wielded his power. He proved his loyalty to her. He contacted a business associate, Jean Luc, an owner, trainer, driver, stabled on race track, and found her new employment and *Toner* a stall. The arrangement worked well. Angel knew the routine. Jean Luc was pleased with her dedication.

CHAPTER FOURTEEN

THE SUN DIPPED BELOW the horizon, and the sky grew dark. The bright light from the street lamps circling the outfield swept over the racetrack. Some birthday, Angel thought, leaning against the tall white board fence inside the paddock. She waited while Jean Luc turned *Toner* behind the mobile starting gate. She looked and spotted one shiny star, alone. "Star light, star bright, first star I see tonight, I wish I may, I wish I might, I wish tonight to see Stephen," she said in her head.

"I've noticed you've distanced yourself from Kerri," a voice said from behind her.

Angel glanced over her shoulder. A young man stood close, wearing a jean jacket over a grey sweat shirt and dark jeans. He was blonde with his hair cut short, grey eyes, and a husky build.

"Pardon?" she asked, clearing her thoughts.

"Hi," he said, smiling. " I'm Simon."

Angel nodded.

"Don't give Kerri a second thought. She has nothing on you."

"I can't believe how wrong I was about her friendship. She was only nice to me 'til I didn't do what she wanted."

"I agree," he said, raising his eyebrows. "Most people only like others when they are giving them what they want, but not all."

"Yeah, I guess."

Simon rubbed the back of his neck. "Do you want to go and have a drink some time?"

"No. I'm not dating anyone at the moment," she said, shaking her head from side to side.

"I don't mean to be pushy. I really would like to know you better. Everyone needs to eat. Don't think of it as a date. Let me buy you supper. It's your call," he said, shrugging.

"Aaaand they'rrrre off," the announcer yelled over the loudspeaker as the starter accelerated, folding the wings of the starter gate.

"Your horse is a cripple," Simon joked.

"My horse has been in the money his last ten starts. *Toner* is due for a win," she said confidently. From her view of the track *Toner* sat third on the rail. Simon's horse trailed hers. His horse proved to be a tough competitor. *Toner* made it to the front. The eight horse field entered the stretch. The spectators filling the grandstand cheered. *Toner* won; Simon's horse finished second.

"Good going, Angel," Simon said over his shoulder, leaving to retrieve his horse from the track.

Angel rushed to the van. She slid the sliding door open and jumped in. The driver drove pulling off the track near the winner's circle. She then slid the door open again and stepped onto the stone dust, and ran to *Toner*. Unhooking the head check, she patted the horse on his strong neck, guiding him in front of the grandstand. She stopped short as Stephen walked through the gate, as handsome as ever, dressed in a soft black leather jacket over a black shirt and new jeans. Sophie cuddled close to him. She glowed, making the most of every feature she had. Stephen pulled away from her hold. He turned half his body toward Angel, running his finger through his dark curly hair. Angel gripped *Toner's* race bridle, wishing the camera man would hurry and take the picture.

The racehorse, blinded from the bright flash, moved side to side. Angel grabbed a better hold, leading the horse and Jean Luc, seated on the sulky, back on the track. She walked to the waiting van and stepped in the open door. The driver headed for the paddock; Stephen and Sophie, the grandstand. Her mind moved as fast as the van did. His memory played in her head. She recalled their first kiss, how passionate his lips felt. She remembered their night alone together, the words he had spoken.

As the driver parked, Angel stepped outside and walked Toner to the test barn. The horse stood tall and proud, nostrils still flaring as she stripped him of his race gear and gave him a hot soapy bath. *Why can't he realize we are perfect for one another*, a voice screamed in her head. If I were older everything would be different.

Angel covered the horse with a cooler blanket and then offered it a drink of water, waiting for the vet to take a urine sample.

Throwing the harness over one shoulder, the wash pail with supplies in her right hand, lead chain in her left, she led the horse back to the stable.

Under a twinkling starry night Angel walked Toner to cool down the horse's system. *Some birthday wish*, she whispered into the night air. She received what she asked for but not the way she expected.

"Angel," Simon's voice broke through her reverie.

Startled, she turned to face him.

"Listen to me," he said once he had her attention. "I would like to know you better. Don't say no, come out with me tomorrow night. There are no races, you have no excuses," he said with his hands in his jean front pockets.

Angel didn't respond. Thinking more with her head than her heart, she intellectualized her recent experiences. Discouraged by what happened and not wanting to be alone any more she took the easy way out, hoping he'd make her happy. "Yeah, I'll go out with you," she agreed as *Toner* nudged his wet nose against her arm.

Simon stepped forward, grinning from ear to ear. He wrapped his arms tight around her torso, pulling her close to him. Angel's body stiffened and he stepped back. "I have to go. I need to apply liniment to my horse's legs and bandage them before I truck the horse to my parents' farm. Pick you up tomorrow night around seven."

Angel nodded in agreement turning toward the barn. She stumbled over her own feet. Stephen stood inside the barn entrance with Sophie on his arm, talking to Jean Luc.

She ignored the couple walking *Toner* into his stall. She paid them no attention, clipping the snap on the water pail to the wall. Her hand trembled as she tossed in a flake of hay, before latching the lock on *Toner's* door.

"Night," she sighed, crossing the shed row. Stephen smiled. His eyes stared deep into hers. She made an effort to smile, but it wasn't good enough, as she left the building.

Angel lay on her bed and closed her eyes. Her head triumphed over her heart but she was sad inside. Defeated by Stephen's rejection, she needed to forget him. He was behind her and Simon was in front of her. Simon wasn't who she wanted, but he was ready and able to love her, so she believed.

Angel tried to sleep but couldn't. She had second thoughts about her decision.

CHAPTER FIFTEEN

NERVOUS, ANGEL SAT BUCKLED in the passenger seat filled with doubt. Simon started the car and then drove off the racetrack grounds. "Have you ever played eight ball?" he asked, steering his car along the main road.

"No," she said, glancing at him, then out the window. The grey sidewalks and paved streets replaced the dying green grass and ditch weeds. The colourful fall trees faded and shopping plazas, street signs and pedestrians emerged.

"Do you know what eight ball is?" he asked.

"No," she sighed.

"Eight ball is a type of pool. The object of the game is one player shoots the solid colours, one through seven; the other, the stripes nine through fifteen. The player who pockets their group of balls first and then pocketing the black eight ball, wins." Simon looked at Angel then back at the road. "You want to stop and shoot a game?"

"Yeah," she said, taking in the sights.

Simon put his turn blinker on, swung off the street into the parking lot, and eased into a free spot. Angel stepped out from the car and followed him toward the Starlight Lounge beside a department store. The people at the long bar that ran the length of the wall from one end to the other, turned and looked at them as they entered the building. She walked close behind Simon across the old brown outdoor carpet-covered floor, past the stage and worn dance floor on her way to the pool tables.

"Where've you been, Simon?" A buxom blonde waitress cooed.

"Working."

"Well, I've missed you around here," she said, flirting.

"Bring me a Coors Light, and gin and ginger ale," he said, brushing her off.

The waitress never gave Angel a second glance, leaving to retrieve their order.

Simon put the correct change into the slot, then shoved the coin holder inward. The pool balls dropped and rolled to the end of the pool table. He grabbed each one and placed them inside a plastic triangle shape. He placed the cue ball on a green felt surface. Turning, he walked to the wall and took two pool cues from the rack. "Are you right or left-handed?" he asked, smiling.

"Right," she answered, taking the pool cue from his hand.

"Your right hand holds the thick end," he said moving closer to her.

"Don't be smart, Simon," Angel said, resting the pool cue on the back rail.

"You're too far away," he said, stepping behind her. "Don't stand too close to the table. Lean in a bit, your left foot should be forward and your right, back," he said, his one shoe against hers guiding her feet. His hands on her hips, he twisted her torso slightly.

"Position your hand to look like a rotated OK sign" he said, stretched over her.

He stood too close for comfort. A cold shiver ran along her spine, following his lead.

"Aim for the middle of the one ball, just below the center," he instructed, stepping away.

Angel focused on her form, practised her stroke, put power in the shot, and pocketed the solid seven.

"Beginner's luck," he said, smiling, paying the large-breasted waitress for their drinks. "Try another solid."

Angel lined up her next shot. She put power in the shot, hit the one ball and slammed the solid three. The ball rolled down the green felt surface, but didn't pocket. Simon eyed the striped twelve ball. He set himself up for the shot, but missed.

"Do you come here a lot?" Angel asked, standing at the head of the table looking for the best shot.

"It's a place to play pool."

"You play often?"

"It's something to do." He gulped the last of his beer and waved the empty bottle in the air at the waitress. Angel and Simon played pool, drank and talked back and forth about not much. She was tired and tipsy leaving the bar. Simon drove bumper to bumper along the twisted city streets to reach the racetrack. He parked the car and shut the motor off. "I had fun, Angel. Do it again some time?" he asked, a little slurred.

"Yeah," she said, reaching for the door handle. She opened the door, stepped onto the dying grass, closing the door behind her.

The next day when Angel finished work Simon was there and every day afterwards. This would be the beginning of a whole chain reaction that would change her life.

CHAPTER SEVENTEEN

SIMON HELD ANGEL'S HAND and squeezed her grip, walking through the turnstiles at the grandstand. "You look more beautiful every day," he whispered without taking his eyes off her.

She looked at his proud face and shook her head, smiling. She kept close to him walking through the three-tier building packed with race fans, heading for the Horseshoe Bar on the ground floor. She took a stool beside him as he ordered their drinks.

"What do you like Simon, the one or four horse in this race?" Bobby asked, standing behind him.

Angel's eyes narrowed, exchanging looks with him. George glanced at her, sinking his hands into his front pockets.

"I don't know, Angel has the program. Are you going to bet?" he asked, turning to face Bobby.

"I bet the four. There's a claim in on the horse."

Simon looked at Bobby's race program, then at the tote-board, then at the program. "At thirty to one—are you nuts!" he exclaimed.

Bobby showed him the ticket.

Angel studied the race program, then checked the tote-board for the payout odds. Ignoring their argument she left them at the bar to wager. She joined the betting line that slowly moved forward.

"Did you pick the winner?" asked a familiar French voice as she walked away from the wicket checking her ticket.

Angel looked into Stephen's sparkling ice-blue eyes. He smiled his bubbly smile. "I like to think so," she said, giggling.

"I can't believe how much you've blossomed since I saw you last," he said, staring at her with an intensity she hadn't seen before.

Without thought, she wrapped her arms around his neck, nuzzling him. Stephen held her tight, and then stepped back. "How have you been?" he asked, smiling.

"Good. You've been gone for a while," Angel said, sighing.

"Making money, Angel. You know it's nothing personal."

"Yeah, I know. You're busy with work," she said, shifting her thoughts and emotions. Her mind told her he was lost to her, but her heart said she'd love him forever.

"Money's power," he said with conviction. You can do anything you want to when you have money."

"I guess," she said, raising her eyebrows.

The announcer over the loudspeaker introduced the horses and drivers parading in front of the grandstand.

"Do you want to watch the race run outside?" he asked, zipping the zipper of his leather jacket.

"Yeah," she said, smiling.

Angel walked with Stephen to the chain link fence. The horses whizzed by them. "What do you want to do, Angel? Do you want to stay here and work your way up the ladder to be a trainer or driver? Do you want to go back home and go to school?" he asked, looking at her.

"Things are good right now," she replied, looking at the pavement, shuffling her feet. "I...I have a boyfriend."

"Who?" he said, surprised.

"Simon Connors," she replied, her eyes focused on the horses jogging by them.

"His family ships in to race?"

"Yeah."

"Simon is not a nice guy, Angel. He has a reputation of being heavy-fisted."

"What! No, that's just gossip. He really does treat me good."

"I don't know about that. Simon is not known to be friendly toward females."

"Your information is wrong!"

"Alright, I believe you. If you say everything is okay, then it is."

"The two horse looks great," she said, changing the subject.

"She's picked third in the race program."

"Ahem," Simon interrupted, clearing his throat suddenly behind them. Angel stood silent. Stephen turned to look over his shoulder. "Did you make your bet, Angel?" Simon asked with suspicion.

"Yeah, but I was talking and didn't see where the horse finished," she said, chuckling.

Simon glared at Stephen. Stephen smirked at him then looked at Angel. "If you ever need anything, please call."

"I will," she said, smiling.

Simon placed his arm around her waist and pulled her tight to his side, walking away.

"You said you were going to bet!" he said, leaving the grandstand.

"I did bet," she said, sighing.

"Did you tell him about us," he asked, giving her a sideway glance.

"Yeah, I told him."

Simon followed her into her tack room venting his concerns. She tried to shake off his accusations. Simon refused to give up. "When were you going to tell me about you and Stephen?"

"What's to tell, we're friends. You're friends with Bobby. I accept that even though he's a complete waste of skin. Quit with your endless questions. You're making something out of nothing. Stephen and I are friends, nothing less, nothing more."

Fed up, Angel wanted the petty argument to be over. She tried to suppress her anger and remain calm, but she blew. "You gotta go. I don't want to listen to you any more!"

"You're trying to play me for a fool!" he screamed, thrusting his face in hers.

Her adrenaline rushed through her veins, not knowing how to deal with his rage.

"Are you blind? Stephen doesn't want you. I give you everything and the thanks I get— you chase some asshole!" he raged, blaming her for the lack of trust between them. He stood inches from her, his face turning the colour of a ripe beet. "You think he'll date a track rat like you!"

Angel stood trembling, unable to speak.

"I give you everything, and you have the nerve to disrespect me. You're just like the rest of the whores out there!"

Simon grabbed her by the hair, pulled her head back, then spit in her face. With force he shoved her onto the cement floor. With swift movement he kicked her several times in the ribs. She attempted to cry, but with the wind knocked out of her, she couldn't catch her breath.

"Fuck you," he yelled, then left, slamming the door behind him.

Angel lay in excruciating pain on the cold cement floor. She didn't know what hurt more, inhaling air or exhaling. She inched her way to the fridge. Her hand shook as she opened the door and removed the bottle of gin. She unscrewed the top, then took a swig trying to ease the horrible ache. She stayed where she fell long after the sun came up. She woke to a loud knock on her door.

"Are you okay, Angel," Jean Luc asked, knocking on the wood.

Even though she knew needed help she couldn't speak.

Jean Luc opened the door. "What happened to you?" he asked, looking in. The day's light poured in blinding her. She put her forearm over her eyes to protect them from the bright sun. "I was jumped at the door last night," she whispered, holding her side.

"What!" he exclaimed, standing in the doorway.

"When I left the Inn last night someone came out of nowhere and laid the boots to me," she said, sighing.

"Wait here," he said, turning, he left.

Where am I going to go? She thought. Angel spotted the empty bottle of gin. She grabbed the long neck and rolled the bottle under the bed. Minutes passed before Jean Luc returned with the track veterinarian. The vet walked to where Angel lay. He knelt beside her and, using both hands, he examined her back. He moved his cold fingers up and down her rib cage asking when it hurt. Withdrawing his hands, he stood.

"Well, I must say, you are one lucky girl. As far as I can find, your ribs are not broken, only bruised."

Jean Luc carefully scooped her into his arms. She hung on with her arms around his neck. Her body flinched from the pain. He laid her on the bed and covered her with the comforter.

"Take this," the vet said, placing one small orange pill in her hand. "The medicine will help you to relax and sleep."

Angel popped the pill into her mouth. Her throat hurt to swallow the drug dry. When the initial pain subsided and her heart rate returned to normal, she stayed under the cover and slept.

Startled, her eyes opened. Simon stood staring at her with a glazed look. He brought an armful of yellow roses and a brown teddy bear with a red bow around the fuzzy neck. She could smell strong liquor on his breath as waves of dizziness and nausea washed through her.

"Forgive me, please. Forgive me!" he begged. "I'm so sorry. I lost my cool. I should never have accused you of cheating." Simon fell to his knees and grabbed her hand. Drifting in and out of wakefulness, she winced in pain. Simon took no notice. "We have something good, don't say we are over. I will have you back. I will. You're the good thing in my life," he rambled.

Almost dead weight, she couldn't believe what he asked. He wanted her to stay in the relationship; she wanted out. Tired, and heavy-lidded, she lay still pretending to be asleep. When Simon finally left she pushed the roses off her bed then struggled to throw the teddy bear against the wall, and sleep descended.

* * * * *

ANGEL GROANED AND BLINKED until her vision cleared. Stephen, wearing a black leather jacket over a blue sweat shirt and jeans was sitting on the edge of the bed. "Jean Luc phoned. He told me you were hurt," he said, stroking her hair. His touch brought her relief. "Did Simon have something to do with this?" he asked.

Her sad eyes penetrated to the very depths of his. "I don't know. It was dark outside," she lied.

"Who was here?" he asked, observing the yellow roses on the floor, then the teddy bear on the opposite side of the room.

"No one that mattered," she said, sighing.

"Do you need to go to the hospital?" I'll drive you."

"No. I'll be fine. The pill I took for the pain is making me groggy."

"I should leave and allow you to rest."

"No, please stay," she said, struggling to sit. "I don't want to be alone."

"I'll stay" he smiled and put his hand on her arm.

Stephen spent an hour adoring how she slept like a peaceful child. He remembered their last night that they had lain together in the dark, waking in her arms, or the taste of her sweet kiss. More than ever he wanted to make her stay at the horse track more comfortable. He stood and took stock of her stuff. He opened the fridge and found inside empty. "This won't do," he said, running his fingers through his hair. He shut the fridge door, then left the tack room. Then, an hour later he returned and filled the fridge with groceries, water and juice. He placed the sweatshirts and socks he bought folded on the couch.

When Angel opened her eyes later she couldn't be happier with his thoughtfulness.

CHAPTER SEVENTEEN

Angel KEPT BUSY, SURROUNDED by people, trying to avoid being alone with Simon. Since his attack on her, he left a gift a day outside her tack room door. She believed his gifts were guilt presents and tossed each and every one in the trash. His apologies were too late. She wished he would go away and leave her be, but he wouldn't.

The summer sun shone bright. Angel's V-neck T-shirt and Levi jean shorts hugged her small curves. Her long hair in a ponytail, the warm breeze blew the loose strands around her face. She hung *Toner's* leather harness in the air clipped between two crossties. She took great care, rubbing the saddle soap with a sponge into the leather to clean the harness. She used a damp cloth to wipe off the excess soap. When she applied the oil to preserve the equipment she glanced out the window. Simon, wearing a brown T-shirt and jeans, sat on the hood of his car talking with Bobby. Then, moments later from the corner of her eye she caught movement. Simon, looking strained, stood in the barn doorway. "Hi, little cutie," he said, smiling from ear to ear.

"Hey," she said, sighing.

"*Toner* raced great last night. You must be happy. The horse came from behind to win the race. Impressive for an old timer," he said, walking closer.

"Yeah," she said, shrugging.

"You're still angry with me, Angel?"

"No. I don't care any more."

"Ahhh, don't be like that. Let me take you for a coffee, we can talk this out," he said, crowding her.

She stepped back, seeing the desperation in his face.

"Give us another chance, Angel. We belong together. It can't be that easy for you to forget all the good times we shared," he said, looking at her, his eyes unblinking. "I really love you. I really miss you! What do you think, want to give s another try?"

Angel pushed her loose hair from her face, standing her ground. "Find someone else, Simon," she said.

"I don't want someone else, I want you!"

Although he frightened her she built up the courage to say what she wanted to say. "Why can't you just let me go?"

"Because I know we can work our problems out if you'd only try," he persisted with a dumb expression on his face.

"We did try but our relationship didn't work. I don't want to argue with you any more, just leave."

Simon overstepped his boundaries seizing her wrist. He leaned close to her face trying to put his lips on hers. He didn't have the look in his eyes for her that Stephen did. Her heart pounded in her chest. She cranked her head to the side. Simon's moist mouth brushed her cheek. He tightened his grip, glancing past her for a brief moment, then back. Someone had walked into the barn at the other end of the shed row.

"Until we meet again, cutie," he said, shoving her hard away from him. He walked out of the stable as if nothing had happened.

Angel trembled stuffing the clean racing gear in the harness bag and closed the zipper. She left the barn, walked across the grass, then entered her tack room. Sitting on the edge of the bed she reached under the box spring, pulled out the bottle of gin, and then unscrewed the lid. She drank from the bottle, and then wiped her mouth with her arm Shaking her head, her eyes watered from the taste. After a few shots of the liquor her breathing and heart slowed to normal. She stared at the door and wondered what would make Simon leave her be. She hoped the confrontation would be their last, but she knew the encounter would not be. Her hand trembled as she tossed two more shots down her throat.

Angel pushed the half-empty gin bottle under the bed. She lay fully clothed on the mattress. Her head swirled and consumed with anxiety and fear, she worried what may come. Traumatized from the attacks gave her a reason to be afraid.

CHAPTER EIGHTEEN

THE SPRINGS SQUEAKED AS Angel sat on the edge of the bed, stretching her arms, yawning. She slipped into her Nike shoes, stood, grabbed her coat from the couch and pulled it over her grey sweatshirt. She found a note slipped under her tack room door. She reached and plucked the piece of paper from the cement floor. She slid her finger across the surface reading the words that leapt from the page. The message read: *Loved you, then I had to kill you, you'll be buried six feet under where no one will find you.*

It took her a minute to process what she read. She froze. Every fibre of her being trembled with fear. "Why won't he leave me alone?" she whispered, tightly crumbling the note in her hands. "Asshole!" she said, tossing the paper over her shoulder.

Her heart thumping, she raised her trembling hand toward the door-knob. *I will not let him scare me into being with him*, she thought. With a strange kind of calm she exited the tack room and looked cautiously, walking to the barn, wondering where he could possibly be. Within minutes of entering the stable she had *Toner* harnessed and ready to race.

The sun set as she headed out of the barn for the horse's first warm up trip. The jogging route along the dirt road was reasonably busy in both directions. Glancing around she spotted Simon's parked vehicle. She refused to allow the rising panic insider her to rule. In the barn she gave *Toner* a quick bath and whistled to empty his bladder. She threw a cooler over the horse to keep him warm and cleaned the stall.

She sat on the tack box, kicking her heels against the front, thinking. She stopped believing that fairy tale love existed and would conquer all. She had yet to experience love without heartache and tears. She had a solid friendship between her and Stephen, but her heart craved more. With Simon she had experienced intense jealousy. Their friendship flourished into a nightmare. The good times had been good; the bad, so bad.

"Get him ready," Jean Luc said in his strong French accent, an hour later, entering the stable.

Startled, Angel looked at him with a puzzled expression.

"Are you okay?" he asked.

"Yeah," she said, standing.

Angel pulled the damp cooler-blanket from *Toner*, tightened the harness straps and replaced the stable halter with the bridle, then attached the reins. Jean Luc sat on the seat of the race bike. He steered *Toner* onto the race track for a second warm up trip.

With a dry cooler-blanket over the left arm and the supplies needed in a large pail in her right hand, Angel headed to the paddock, and then put what she carried in the horse's race stall. Outside, she leaned against the tall white board fence, glancing around. The bright light from the street lamps that circled the outfield swept over the track. The skin on her arms prickled spotting Simon lurking in the shadows.

Jean Luc steered *Toner* off the track.

Angel took a deep breath, leading the horse inside the paddock to the race stall. She gave *Toner* a few pats trying to calm her nerves. Alert to her surroundings, she loosened the race gear and put the proper head number and saddle pad with *Toner's* post-position on the animal's harness.

The horse stood still and silent in the crossties as people bustled about in the building. About ten minutes prior to post-time a loud crackle of the microphone came over the loudspeaker. "The horses are called to the post parade," the announcer said.

Angel strapped the race bike onto either side of the harness, then added the bridle. She led the horse out of the building. Jean Luc hopped onto the seat of the race bike.

Angel stood by the white board fence as the field of horses paraded in front of the grandstand. The track announcer introduced the horses, drivers, trainers, and owners. She smiled to herself when he said Stephen's name.

One minute to post and in post position order, the horses headed toward the mobile starting gate. The official starter accelerated. Around the paddock turn the wings of the starting gate folded. "Annnd, they're off," the announcer yelled over the loudspeaker.

Toner raced in the pocket then pulled and moved through the pack. The horse showed great performance and finished second.

Angel stood, stunned, when the track announcer said someone purchased *Toner*. Her heart visibly broken she walked to the race stall, retrieved the cooler-blanket and wash pail. She headed to the test barn. Jean Luc had snapped the horse to the crossties. The new owners allowed her enough time with *Toner* to strip him of his racing gear. She threw the harness over her shoulder, picked up the wash pail with one hand and the shaft of the race bike in the other, she headed for Jean Luc's stable.

Back at the barn Angel placed the sulky beside the jog bikes, dropped the wash pail at the door, hung the harness outside the empty stall, and then walked away. She stepped around the corner of the barn. Her heart lurched. Simon, wearing a jean jacket over a black sweater and basic five-pocket jeans, stood outside her tack room door. "How's it going?" he asked.

Angel sighed. "Leave me alone."

"We need to straighten things between us," he said in an overly calm voice.

"There's nothing left to be straightened," she said, stepping back.

"You'll change your mind," Simon persisted, smirking.

"No, I won't!"

"There's not a relationship that doesn't have hard times," he continued, stepping forward. "You're my everything. You make me feel things I've never felt before. You are all I think about. It can't be too late. I don't want to give up on us!"

Angel stood, trembling from head to toe. She feared the anguish in his voice.

"What am I supposed to do, Angel? I love you so much. I need you, you mean so much to me," he rambled.

She shook her head, looking at the ground. She couldn't believe they ended right back where their conversation had started. "I'm sorry, Simon, but I don't feel the same. I care about you," she lied, "but I don't love you."

Simon looked at her with eyes widened. He charged toward her and gripped her wrist, squeezing tight. He swung her around. From behind her he reached his hand to her face. In slow motion, she caught her reflection on the edge of the blade. All she could do was stand, paralyzed with fear.

Simon's hand trembled holding the sharp knife to her throat. "I want you to listen. You won't listen. You walk by me like I'm invisible," he said, teeth clenched, spitting the words in her ear.

Angel stood, shocked. Tears filled her eyes. She swallowed hard. With her arm locked in his powerful grip, he ran the edge of the blade along her skin, slicing the flesh. Warm blood droplets sprouted from the wound.

"Please don't do this, Simon. You're making a mistake!" she begged.

"I love you!" he said with the sharp point of the knife aimed at her jugular vein.

"So you're going to kill me," she said, swallowing hard, trying not to cry.

"With one stroke," he said with venom. "I could take your life like you have taken mine!"

Angel, scared and confused, attempted not to move, being held against her will. Her mind spun with possibilities to escape. She noticed headlights and the sound of a motor wheel in front of Jean Luc's barn, and then park. The truck door opened. "I'll be right back," her boss said. He slammed the door shut and walked across the grass in her direction.

Simon released her arm, pushed her hard, and vanished into the dark. Her heart thumping, she fell into the door.

"Hey, Angel," her boss said, smiling. His eyes fixed on her. "Are you okay?"

"Yeah, I tripped," she said, forcing herself to her feet.

"Are you sure you're alright?"

"Yeah, I'm fine," she whispered.

"I forgot to pay you," he said, pulling an envelope from his inner pocket. "Good night?" he questioned, handing her pay cheque to her.

"Thanks," she whispered. She opened the tack room door and stepped inside. Terrified, she jammed two butter knives into the door-frame and pushed in on the doorknob to secure the lock.

Angel sat in the dark on the cold cement floor, her knees pulled to her chin. She held her face in her hands and sobbed. She could hear her heart pound in her ears as her mind attempted to process what just happened. She couldn't believe her life had been at risk, looking at the blood droplets seeping through her grey sweat shirt.

Angel reached under the bed and removed a half-full bottle of gin. She screwed off the lid and gulped a mouthful of the liquor. Her face screwed up from the taste. After a few more drinks she curled in the foetal position and tried to sleep. She had horrible nightmares, waking in a cold sweat.

CHAPTER NINETEEN

Angel STEPPED OUT OF the grey block building, a bundle of nerves. She flinched at every sound she heard, crossing the empty parking lot. She popped a breath mint into her mouth to disguise the smell of liquor on her breath, walking along the side of the dirt road. She shivered at the sound of a motor crawling behind her. Stephen stopped his truck, leaned and opened the passenger window. "Hi, Angel," he said, smiling. "Will you join me for lunch?"

"Yeah," she answered, beaming.

"Get in then."

She climbed into the truck thinking how she loved his French accent. The sound made her feel good. Stephen gripped the steering wheel with one hand, exited the back stretch, and then swung his vehicle onto the main road. He looked at her then out the windshield. "Anywhere special you want to eat?" he asked.

"Pizza would be great," she said, moving her hair away from her face.

"You're in desperate need of a haircut," he said, glancing at her then back at the two-lane highway.

"Yeah," she answered, observing the scenery fly by.

A few minutes later Stephen pulled off into a strip mall. He eased the truck into an empty parking spot and killed the engine. "We'll start here," he said, opening the door. He stepped on to the pavement and walked toward the store front. Angel opened the passenger door, slid out of the vehicle, then followed close beside him.

He held the door open for her. The small bell above their heads announced their arrival. Angel looked around the salon in awe at the many exotic haircut prints on the white walls of the clean, bright building.

"May I help you?" a well dressed, top heavy woman asked in a strong French accent, sitting at the reception desk.

"My friend needs a haircut, nothing wild," he said, smiling.

"I have time" A small woman with unnatural bleached blonde, big hair, announced, standing with her hands clasped at her waist.

"Name?" the receptionist asked.

Once Stephen gave her the required information, he sat on the red leather sofa in the waiting area.

The hairdresser waved for her to follow. Angel walked to the washbasin and sat in the chair.

"That's one nasty cut you have. How did you ever wound yourself on your neck?" the hairdresser asked, putting the red protective cape on her.

Angel tried to cover the slice with her hand, noticing Stephen take an interest in the conversation. She leaned her head back, closed her eyes, and enjoyed the woman's fingers massaging her scalp. The crème rinse, the scent of ripe strawberries filled the air. With a warm, white towel wrapped tight around her wet hair, Angel moved to the hairdresser's station. The small woman with the bleached blonde hair took her scissors in hand and began to cut, a little here, a little there. She wisped the bangs and sides thin. The length she feathered. She dried the style with a blow dryer. When she removed the red protective cape bits of hair spilled to the floor. Angel sat in the chair in front of the mirror smoothing her hair. She couldn't be more pleased. "How do I look, Stephen?" she asked, standing and shaking her head of hair.

"Perfect," he said, paying the hairdresser. "Let's have lunch. I'm starved," he joked, pulling the door open for her.

Angel walked into the Italian restaurant a few stores down from the beauty salon. Stephen pulled out a chair at the two-seater table for her to sit, and then sat across from her. "Would you like a drink from the bar?" the waitress asked with pen and paper in hand.

Angel glanced toward the bartender, pouring a draft from the taps at the oak bar, laughing with the customers.

"I'll have a gin and ginger ale, please," she said, turning to the waitress.

"She'll settle for a ginger ale and I will have a coffee," Stephen said, interrupting.

Silent, she sat back in the chair reading the menu. The waitress returned with their drinks, then left with their food order.

"Thank you for my new style. I love it," she said, fluffing the sides of her auburn hair.

Stephen's eyes narrowed. "Where did the bruise around your wrist and the small but deep cut on your throat come from?" he asked.

"What—" she dithered, placing her one hand in her lap and the other tugging her hair over the wound.

"Are you still involved with Simon?"

"No," she said, sitting back in the chair, arms folded across her chest.

"Have you phoned your parents?"

"Yeah, same old conversation. They want me home and enrolled in school. I don't know, maybe it's time for me to pack up and leave," she said, sighing. Her reality held her back from what she really wanted to do, stay. Simon complicated her life. He had beaten her down. She couldn't mentally handle the conflict she found herself in.

"I'm going to claim two horses and I wondered if you'd groom them for me. If you decide you want your trainer's license I'll teach you all I know, Angel," he said, leaning on the table.

She couldn't hide her joy. Her eyes sparkled, grinning from ear to ear. "You want me to work for you?" she asked.

"If you want."

The waitress brought their food to the table. She laid a slice on each of their plates, then left.

"Looks great!" Stephen said, eyeing his slice.

"Smells good, too," Angel agreed. She picked up her slice, blew on the toppings, then bit into the cheesy goo.

"I would like you to do one thing for me," he said, looking at her.

She swallowed a mouthful of pizza. "What's that?"

"I need you to slow down on your drinking."

She looked at him and refrained from answering, shifting in her seat.

"Over the past few weeks you've become tense and irritable, Angel. I'm not judging you."

"I only have a few drinks to unwind, Stephen."

He stared at her without a word said.

"Alright, I'll slow down," she said, attempting a compromise.

"I'm worried about you. Has Simon threatened violence toward you over the break-up?"

Agitated, she picked the toppings off her second pizza slice, one by one. "It's complicated," she said, giving him a wry look.

Stephen stopped short pressuring her for an answer. He didn't want to upset her more than she was. He cherished their friendship. He could talk to her. Her genuine interest and consideration for him resulted in a strong bond between them. He took the pressure off. He looked at his watch, then waved to the waitress for the check.

"It's five o'clock. We should head back to the race track," he announced.

Stephen paid the bill. Angel smiled to herself walking close beside him to the truck. He waited for cars to pass and pulled onto the two-lane highway. She chatted about nothing much while he drove. He put the signal on, then braked and aimed for the racetrack's long laneway.

In the back stretch a sudden terror consumed her entire being.

Stephen stepped out from the truck and stood. "Who did this, Angel?" he demanded.

She shut the passenger door behind her. Silent, she stared at her front door kicked in.

"Angel!" he shouted.

She said nothing, not knowing what to say.

"I assume this mess is compliments of Simon?" he asked, his eyes taking in the tack room.

She walked over to him. Her eyes scanned the clothes thrown about. She could smell Simon's smell. His cologne and Irish Spring soap lingered in the air.

Stephen stepped over the clothes on the floor. He picked up the crumpled note from the white table and read the words: Loved you, then I had to kill you, you'll be buried six feet under, where no one will find you, then twice, the third more slowly. "What is this?" he demanded, voice raised.

"Don't read that!" she said in a panic-stricken voice.

"Who wrote this?" he said, waving the piece of paper at her.

She gave him a weary look.

"Did Simon write this?"

For a minute she believed he might leave. She needed him to stay. "I don't know how someone who cared for me so much can be so evil. In the beginning he had been a perfect gentleman. He opened the car door and pulled out chairs for me. I don't know what I've done to him to deserve such rage," she said, fighting the tears. Their eyes met. Stephen stepped closer to her. She slipped into his arms. "It's okay, I'm here," he said, hugging her tight to him. *For now*, she thought.

Stephen pressed his lips against her hair. Faced with the moment of her truth, she broke. Sobbing, she told him everything Simon had done to her.

CHAPTER TWENTY

Stephen SHIFTED HIS POSITION on the couch. He lay awake thinking. He concentrated on a solution, not the problem. With every kiss, hug and conversation he found himself falling in love. He decided to partner with Angel in business and in pleasure. Her heartache signalled to him that the time had come to move Sophie out, and her in. His choice brought him a sense of freedom.

Angel lay stretched under the comforter on the bed, sleeping. Her thoughts drifted to what Simon had done. Scenes from the past haunted her dreams. She awoke startled. The soft full moon's light flooded the room. Her eyes darted from the door, window and four walls.

"Another nightmare?" Stephen asked.

"Yeah," she said, sighing.

"Maybe you should call the police, Angel. You need a restraining order to keep him at bay."

She turned and lay on her side to face him. Her head rested on her hand. "I should, but I don't want to do more to upset him," she said, yawning.

"Simon's actions have very little to do with you, Angel," Stephen countered, annoyed. "He has control issues. If you call the police and make a report you'll put the control back in your court. It's your choice."

"Yeah, I guess. Would you drive me Friday afternoon? I have to work tomorrow during the day, then race a horse at night."

"Certainly. Now close your eyes and sleep," he said, smiling.

"I'd sleep better if you were beside me," she said with a shy smile.

He didn't need to be invited twice. He joined her in the bed, locking his arm tight around her. Her head settling on his shoulder, safe in his embrace, she slept knowing he meant to her what she meant to him.

CHAPTER TWENTY-ONE

ANGEL DRESSED IN CLEAN jeans, black sweat shirt, and Nikes, turned her head. Stephen, his breath slow and shallow, lay sprawled on the bed wearing yesterday's clothes, sleeping. *Handsome and desirable*, she thought, hypnotized by the man.

Bundled against the chill, her hand on the door knob, the squeak of springs on the bed startled her. She glanced over her shoulder. Stephen lay looking at her. "Morning," he said, his voice scratchy.

"Morning," she said, her eyes on his sleepy face.

"Come here," he said, patting the sheet. Silent, she walked the short distance and sat on the edge of the bed. His hand framed her face. "I like looking at you," he murmured.

Her cheeks flamed red and her eyes fell to the cement floor.

"Don't be shy. You're beautiful," he said.

She glanced at him, then away.

"You're amazing. I want you, Angel," he said, lifting her chin with his hand.

"Why?" she said, staring into his cheerful ice-blue yes.

"Why not? Your flaws are not all that bad," he said, smiling.

She shook her head from side to side, grinning.

Stephen slipped his arms around her and lifted her to him. She tumbled, swinging beneath him on the bed. A tangle of arms and legs thrashed about as she struggled to free herself.

"Get off me," she said, laughing. "I have to go to work!"

"No, you're staying here with me," he said, smiling as she attempted to wriggle free.

"Seriously. I have to feed the horses," she said half under him.

"Really?" Humour sparkled in his eyes.

"Really!"

He pulled her close, lowered his head and closed his mouth on hers. Her heart thumping against her rib cage she trembled as his mouth found hers again.

Stephen swung her in a circle. "Fine then, go to work," he said, smiling.

Angel could read his eyes filled with love and believed their relationship had worked itself out. She drew a deep breath, then exhaled, running her hand through his curly black hair. She gave him a hard hug, her head tucked on his shoulder.

"Go to work before I change my mind," he whispered into her hair, releasing his hold on her.

"Okay, okay, I'll go."

She rose to her feet and brushed her wrinkled coat and jeans, and walked to the door. "See you later," she said over her shoulder.

"Yes, go to work," he said, sitting.

"Okay. I'm gone," she opened the door and left.

Angel walked *Misieur Riches* from his stall. The horse stood quiet snapped to the crossties in the alley. She used the pitchfork to remove the manure and wet straw from the horse's bedding, then tossed the soiled straw into the wheelbarrow. She wheeled the full barrow outside and dumped the contents into the assigned area. She then added fresh straw, enough for a thick bedding, then removed the water bucket from the wall. She scrubbed the inside clean, filled the bucket with cold water, then snapped it to the wall in the empty stall. She tossed in a flake of hay, and then walked *Misieur Riches* into his home for the day. She did the same for the two other horses she cared for before she harnessed the animals and jogged them around the oval track for their daily exercise.

The back stretch consumed with activity, she had no stress or worries.

Her day's work completed, dirty from the stone dust blowing in her hair and face, she headed for the showers. Behind the locked door she stripped down to her skin, stepped in, shut the shower door and turned on the taps. The hot water sprayed on her soothing her sore muscles. Angel washed, smiling to herself knowing her dream had turned into reality. Stephen shared her love. His thoughtfulness permeated their friendship. He was in her life to stay.

Angel dried herself, then dressed in warm clothes. She rolled the shampoo, soap and dirty clothes in the towel, then exited the grey-brick building. The door closed behind her. She stopped, a little panicked, surveying her surroundings. The white clouds in the baby blue sky stood still. A strong, sharp wind blew and twirled the fiery autumn leaves on the ground. The nose of Simon's car stuck out beside the closest long Indian red horse barn. Angel stood and tried to deliberate on how to proceed. She struggled with herself, trying to muster the courage to walk along the dirt road to her tack room.

"Are you alright, Angel?" Stephen asked seeming to appear out of nowhere.

She looked over her shoulder. He had changed into a clean dark blue sweatshirt and jeans. Their eyes met. "I am now that you're here," she replied, smiling with relief.

Stephen moved to face her. He placed his fingers under her chin and directed his mouth on hers. Her arms wrapped tight around his neck, she rose to her toes and took his mouth with hers, kissing him slow and steady. He pulled away only to hold her in his arms.

"Thank you, Stephen, for being you," she whispered against his cheek. They drew apart.

"You look tired," he said, tucking a strand of hair behind her ear.

"Yeah, I am," she sighed.

"Come with me." He placed his arm around her waist, pulling her close. She travelled along the dirt road scanning the area. She approached the tack room on pins and needles anticipating Simon had a next move. Stephen opened the door and she stepped inside.

Angel sank onto the mattress. Stephen lay close beside her, holding her in his embrace. His warm breath against her neck. She closed her eyes and tried not to think of Simon's threat. She couldn't sleep, reliving the terror of him with the edge of the sharp blade to her throat.

"Wake up, Angel," Stephen said, his hand on her hip he gave her a light shove.

"I'm awake," she said, rolling onto her back, staring at the ceiling.

"You're scared, aren't you?" he asked, shifting his body.

She waited a long moment, then decided to talk. "Simon's threats are real. I know what he's capable of."

"Don't be afraid," He said, leaning, then kissed her hair.

Yeah, right, she thought. She rose and slipped her socked feet into her Nikes. Ten minutes later she walked *Misieur Riches* out of the box stall into the alley, then snapped the horse to the crossties. She brushed the horse's soft brown coat. A light dust cloud appeared with every flick. She used the body brush to smooth down the hair, then combed the mane and tail. With a clean towel she wiped the animal's coat to bring out a shine. She pulled the race gear from the harness bag. The forest green saddle pad matched the fuzzy material velcroed over the buxton martingale that would hold the harness from slipping. She placed a clean cloth onto the crupper, then slipped the racing gear over the horse's long tail, pulled the harness into place, and buckled the belt loosely around *Misieur Riches'* girth. Stephen bent over, cleaning the horse's hooves with the hoof pick. Then he hung the hopple straps front and back, and buckled the hopples to them. Angel braided both the mane and tail. She replaced the stable halter with the race bridle. Outside, the brisk wind blew her hair as she held the horse while Stephen hooked the sulky on to either side of the harness. Jean Luc sat on the seat and left the barn area to go the first mile.

Stephen fed and hayed the remaining horses in the stable as Angel topped the water buckets that hung on the stall walls. She tossed a cooler-blanket over one arm, and, with her right hand, grabbed the wash pail with the supplies inside.

With twilight sky growing darker, the bright light from the street lamps circled the outfield, and swept over the back stretch. *Life is good*, Angel thought as she walked beside him.

"Would you move in with me tonight?" he suddenly asked.

She swung to face him. "You want to take me home with you–to your home?" she questioned, eyebrows raised.

"Yes," he said, grinning.

"I'll go now and pack my bag!"

"Not so fast, baby, you have a horse to race."

Angel dropped everything she carried. The contents clinked hitting the ground. She leaped off her feet and onto his body, wrapping her limbs tight around him, her mouth moved warm over his. She stood and steadied herself, smiling. "The sooner we start, the sooner we can go home," she said, giggling.

Still beaming, she entered the paddock close to him. She placed the wash pail in the race stall, then threw the cooler-blanket over the side of the wall.

Stephen laid a hand over hers and turned his so their fingers linked, walking beside her. They exited the building to meet Jean Luc.

Jean Luc steered his horse leaving the oval racetrack and pulled the horse to a stop. He hopped off the sulky and hooked the lines to the harness. "He warmed up nice, Stephen," he said, smiling.

"I agree. He's picked as the favourite in the program," Stephen replied, loosening the stop ties around the shaft of the sulky on either side of the harness.

Angel led the horse into the paddock minus the sulky. She walked the large animal to the race stall, removed the bridle and replaced the gear with a stable halter.

"Will you be okay if I go outside with Jean Luc to watch the next race, Angel?" Stephen asked, walking the sulky to the back of the stall.

"Yeah, no worries," she said, scraping the horse's coat to remove the sweat.

"See you soon," he said with a wink.

Vapour rose from the nostrils of the harnessed horse as she picked up the two front legs and removed them from the hopples. With a clean towel she wiped the dirt from the inside of the equipment. She tossed the cooler-blanket over the animal's hot coat and waited for Stephen to return, truly content she would have her happy ever after.

"Thirteen minutes to post," a voice crackled over the loudspeaker.

"Would you like a coffee, Angel," Stephen asked, returning.

"Yeah, that would be great," she said, replacing the stable halter with the race bridle.

*   *   *   *   *

J EAN LUC TIED THE leather straps on either side of the harness around the shafts. He unhooked the lines, hopped on the seat, then put his boots in the stirrups. Angel led the horse out of the paddock. She reached for the over check that pulled *Misieur Riches'* head in place, then snapped the ring to the harness.

"You don't have a head-pole on the horse. He needs one to race. Wait for Stephen to come back before you go to the barn," Jean Luc said, facing her jogging by.

Damn. The horse will bear in on the turns during the race without the equipment, she thought, leaving the paddock area. The street lamps lining the dirt road, racetrack, and grandstand, lit the dark night. She slid the huge wooden door open, walked in and grabbed the needed head pole from the wall. The fall leaves outside rustled, blowing in on the ground. The horse in the stall beside her stuck his head over the door. His ears perked, his neck and head jerked upward, stepping from side to side on the dry straw. Angel turned and stumbled with fright. Simon stood in the open doorway. His hair tangled, his clothes wrinkled, his eyes red for lack of sleep. Angel trembled, mesmerized by the rifle he held in his right hand, finger on the trigger.

Angel wished she had been more careful, trying to keep her composure. *I have to get away from him, but how,* she wondered, panicked..

Sad, frustrated and rejected, Simon spoke his truth, no matter the consequences. "I've been waiting for us to meet face to face," he said, his voice grim. "When were you going to tell me there are three people in this relationship?"

"What?" she said, eyes wide.

"I knew I wasn't the only one, you've been dating Stephen."

"No. He's my friend!"

Simon stared at her with disdain. "Sure. A friend with benefits. The whole time you were with me you were with him!" he said, raising the steel barrel of the gun straight at her.

"No," she stammered, "that's not how it was."

"This is the last time you make a fool out of me. You're a liar!"

Scared, she stepped backwards away from him. *This can't be happening*, she thought. *I don't want to die.*

"Get in the car," he demanded.

Angel believed he had lost his mind, scanning the back stretch. He walked closer and grabbed her on the shoulder. "Get in the car!"

With no one near she took the practical and simplest approach and complied.

Simon led her to his car and forcefully pushed her inside. He sat in the driver's seat, laid the rifle lengthwise on his lap, finger on the trigger. He started the engine. With his coat over the steel barrel he drove them off the horse track grounds. He continued to drive and torment her. His feelings derailed his thinking. One minute he'd be calm, then he wouldn't be. "What did I do to make you go, Angel?" he said, glancing at her then out the windshield.

"Nothing," she stuttered.

"What can I do to make you come back? I need you. I can't be without you. I've never felt this way about anyone! Why don't you love me any more?" he screamed, slamming his fist into the seat beside her. "What am I supposed to do?"

Angel flinched, but she had no plans for their union to lead to a reconciliation. She decided to go head to head with him. "Don't you think it's a little too late for us? Our chance has come and gone. You can't force me to love you so get over it!" she said, facing him, then away.

"To think I thought you were different, you slut," he said through his teeth. With the combination of his physical strength and rage, he grabbed her by the hair and slammed her face hard onto the dashboard. As her head flung back, he slammed the side of her head against the window. Her sight blurred as blood gushed from her nose. "Oh, God, what have you done?" she cried in horrible pain.

Simon looked at her with satisfaction, then at the road. "Not so mouthy now, are you bitch?"

"I hate you!" she cried, tears flowing down her cheeks.

He reached and grabbed a handful of hair, yanking her head back and forth. Her lips crashed into the gear-shift. "You're not my favourite person either," he grated.

Angel slid to the floor on the passenger side of the car, sobbing, her head in her hands. He wheeled his vehicle in and out of traffic. There was not a word said between them until he parked the car. He gestured for her to come out. Blurry-eyed, she looked at her surroundings. The long laneway, large field-stone home, open field and the silhouette of horses standing in the background she realized she had arrived at Simon's family farm.

A black Labrador, wagging his tail, appeared. Simon ignored the dog leading her through the open field with the rifle pointed at her back. Trusting, the black Lab followed .Angel, her face aching, deep red blood flowing from her nose, looked at the bright full moon in the heavens. *I don't want to die. I can't die*, she prayed.

She moved among the dried weeds. "No one's coming to save you," Simon grated, jabbing the rifle into her spine.

He gripped her arm, whirled her to face him, trying to mess with her head. "I should have slit your throat when I had the chance," he said, his tone icy.

She wiped the blood from her nose and lip onto her jeans. The black Lab smelled the red stain. He sat and stared with a curious look at her. Filled with grief about what would come, she patted the dog's soft hair on his head. "I'm tired of going around in circles with you. Nothing I've done has driven you to your destruction," she said, facing Simon. You hate yourself because you keep making the same mistakes that drove you to your actions, she thought.

Despite his doom and gloom preaching he had lost his hold on her. She didn't try to overcome her situation with force or anger. She challenged him to take responsibility for his actions. "You love me so much you are going to kill me," she said in a calm tone.

"It kills me inside to know you are with someone else. How else do I rid myself of the pain?" he said, lowering his voice.

"Nobody says love is easy. Nothing in love is fair. When things don't work out with someone, find someone else!" she said, asserting her thoughts.

"I don't want someone else, I want you! Why can't you love me?" Simon demanded, pointing the rifle at her. "I don't want to go on another day without you. If I can't have you, no one will!"

Angel believed she fought a losing battle. He would either kill her or stalk her forever. "You do damage to me, you only do it to yourself. If you take my life, you take your own," she said, sighing. "Am I worth spending the rest of your life behind bars? Because, unless you are planning to use one of those bullets on yourself, that's exactly where you will end up, jail."

Something inside her shifted. Somehow she separated herself from her experience. A new strength came over her reaching her breaking point. She woke from her nightmare and decided to walk away. Accepting her fate, the hardest part was over. She stood with pride, inhaling and exhaling a deep breath of air. "Do what you must, but I'm going home," she said.

"Why should I let you go?" he asked, pointing the rifle at her, looking for a reaction. She gave none.

Her heart pounded. She turned, and put one foot in front of the other. Simon stepped forward, crunching in the dried grass as he thumbed the hammer of the rifle. He took aim for his line of fire. She remained calm and centered, walking. He fired—boom, the shell popped from the chamber and the next bullet popped in. Her entire body flinched from the noise of the shot and sharp yelp. Up ahead to the right, the black Lab staggered and fell on the brown grass. Blood poured fast from his head. A cold tremor rippled through her as tears streamed down her cheeks. Helpless and in fear for her own life, she kept on the move. She crossed the open field, past the barn, and the main house, down the long drive, through the gate to the main highway. She stepped into the ditch out of sight. She walked to the police station to file a complaint against Simon. She didn't know how else to make him stop.

CHAPTER TWENTY-TWO

T HE SUN HAD COME up in the east by the time all was said and done. The police would arrest Simon and charge him with kidnapping, assault with a weapon, and forcible confinement. The officers removed the responsibility from Angel.

At the police station, alone, she sat on a wooden bench with her head in her hands. Tired and blood stained, memories of what happened played in her mind like a horror film. She didn't notice Stephen enter the building. He walked over to where she sat. "Angel," he said, extending his hand to her. She set her eyes on him, stood and threw her arms tight around his neck. Her entire body exhaled as she released a deep sigh.

"I was stunned by your sudden disappearance," he said, his lips against her hair. "Back at the barn I tried to determine what happened. I saw the head-pole on the floor and the sliding door open. I assumed you had an unexpected visit from Simon."

"It's over now. I'm fine," she said, looking at him. Her arms around his neck, she leaned her lower half against him.

"You are either one very brave woman, or foolish, to do what you did," he said, standing with his hands resting on the small of her back. "Is your nose broken?"

"No," she said, sighing, "the cartilage is torn. My nose will heal." She lovingly studied his handsome, sharp, crystal blue eyes and genuine smile.

"You're beautiful. I love you, Angel. Come home with me to stay. I promise to care for you and keep you safe," he said, running his finger along her chin.

Angel buried her face against his shoulder. "Yes, I love you, too," she said.

Stephen slipped his hand over hers, linking his fingers with hers. She leaned her head against his shoulder. They walked side by side toward the exit.

A great happiness bubbled from within her. The spark between them fanned over time and developed into a burning fire. Her love story had a fairy tale ending. She learned through her experience with relationships that love can mystify and there are no straight lines in love, only the mystery of the curve.

ABOUT THE AUTHOR

ANGIE SKELHORN

I am the fifth child born into a farming family located south of Peterborough, ON. Canada.

The domestic animals as well as the wildlife found at the farm held much amusement for me during my childhood. Living in the country performing seasonal tasks added much to my appreciation of nature.

I ventured forth to discover myself at the tender age of fourteen. My journey took me to the Ottawa area. Initially I found employment as a horse groomer, followed by twenty-plus years as a waitress. After sampling many of life's pleasures and pitfalls witchcraft captured my interest. I returned to the family farm where I became fascinated with witchcraft; the lifestyle, beliefs customs and traditions.

I found the teaching of the craft offered a positive blueprint for living. My stories are moulded somewhat after my life, but are not a true to any type of memoir.

My love of nature, my imagination, and the desire to share the knowledge of the benefits of witchcraft are obvious in my writing. You may visit my at http://witchskel.com

Made in the USA
Charleston, SC
09 June 2011